A TIME FOR US "will win Miss Hale many new readers." (Buffalo Courier Express.) **Corliss Mitchell,** who defied her father to love struggling young Reese Sheridan, waited hopefully for that time. But Reese wanted success first – and Jenny Kaldner was the key. Combining

ARLENE HALE

A Time for Us

Curley Publishing, Inc.
South Yarmouth, Ma.

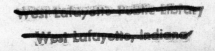

Library of Congress Cataloging-in-Publication Data

Hale, Arlene.
   A time for us / Arlene Hale.—South Yarmouth, MA. :
J. Curley & Associates, 1977, c1972.
   364 p. : 22 cm.
   Large print ed.
   ISBN 0–89340–049–1
   1. Large type books.   I. Title.
   [PZ4.H1618 Ti 5]   813'.5'4   76–45207
   [PS3515.A262]   MARC
   Library of Congress   76[88]rev

Published in Large Print by arrangement with Little, Brown and Company in the U.S.A. and Blanche C. Gregory, Inc. for the U.K. and Commonwealth.

Distributed in Great Britain, Ireland and the Commonwealth by CHIVERS LIBRARY SERVICES LIMITED, Bath BA1 3HB, England

4/9₂ CURLEY 6.95

Printed in Great Britain

"For the members of the Hale Clan
and the root of us all,
Mom"

The characters
in this story are fictitious.
Any resemblance
to persons living or dead is
purely coincidental.

A Time for Us

I

The door to Corliss Mitchell's bedroom was closed. Locked. She wanted no one wandering in without invitation. The bags on the bed were nearly packed. With one last, quick check, she snapped them shut. Her hands were trembling. Was it really about to happen? After all this time? Would this really be her last night in this room?

Glancing at her watch, she saw that it was nearly midnight. Snapping off the light, she opened the door slowly, noiselessly. She listened. There wasn't a sound in the house. Her father's room at the end of the hall was quiet and no light showed under the door. It wasn't likely that Martha and Samuel Worth, who lived in a small apartment at the rear of the house, were up either. They always retired promptly at ten o'clock.

1

She took the bags, walked quickly down the hall, and let herself out. In the garage, she stowed them in her car, pausing now and then to listen and watch for lights coming on in the house. Done! Now all she must do was wait for the morning.

This, she soon learned, was the hardest part of all. She tried sleeping, but it was impossible. Three times she reached for the phone beside her bed to call Elizabeth Lane, her best friend and co-worker at the lab. Elizabeth knew all her hopes and dreams. Elizabeth would be as pleased and happy as she was. But Reese had wanted it kept secret. So she wouldn't call Elizabeth, even though every nerve in her body was tuned to a high pitch. Excitement wove itself in and around her heart, tying it in silver knots.

Tomorrow a dream was going to come true. A dream that had started years ago. She smiled as she remembered that day when she had first seen Reese Sheridan.

Roberts Mill was a landmark in the area, a proud memento of yesterday tucked away inside Willow Woods, and for as long as she could remember it had been her favorite place. She had been a tall, long-legged girl that day, day-dreaming away the hours in her own private little Eden. What a shock it had been to look up and see the strange boy with shaggy black hair and burning eyes.

"Who are you?" she asked.

"Reese Sheridan. I know you. You're Mitchell's daughter."

She laughed. It was sort of fun to be "Mitchell's" daughter. Her father was a power and an influence in the neighboring city of Seabourne. "What of it?" she asked.

Reese Sheridan lifted his bony shoulders in a shrug. "Are you going to tell on me for being here? I just sort of sneaked in."

She giggled. "That's silly. Anybody can come here."

"Only they don't."

"Then, why did you?"

He looked around him, chin up defiantly. "Because I like it here. Because I

3

wanted to."

"I won't tell. Where do you live? How did you get here?"

"I live in Seabourne. I pedaled out on my bike. And I come from near the river-front."

He had been defensive and angry. But exciting. Different from anyone she had ever known. Being Mitchell's daughter had its drawbacks as well as its advantages. Her parents tended to shelter her. Reese Sheridan was intriguingly and instantly different. There was something bold and untamed about him.

"Did they really use this old mill once, long ago?" he asked.

"My great-great-grandfather brought wheat here to have it ground into flour."

"Wow!" he said softly.

"Come on, I'll show you. It's my favorite place. I know all about it."

They had explored the mill. She showed him where a loose board in the floor had to be carefully side-stepped, where her grandfather had carved his initials, and where the violets grew in the

4

damp shadows, and field mice had nested.

That day had been one of the most adveturesome in her life. Reese dared fate and tempted the devil, and she soon found herself dogging his footsteps, doing impetuous things, swept up into his reckless world.

They arranged to meet there whenever they could. Their friendship grew and blossomed, a secret thing. They swam in the cool green pool by the mill, and she followed him in impossibly high dives that could have broken her neck. They crawled up into trees and swung from nimble branches. They shouted, ran, chased rabbits, clambered constantly over the old mill, and laughed like fools over nothing.

Then there were quiet times, stretched in the sun on their backs, studying the sky and talking about deep things -- and what Reese would be one day.

"An important man," he'd said with his teeth clenched. "The kind people will call sir, and nod to, and give a tip of their hat. And I'll have money – I'll be a millionaire."

"I'd rather be happy," she said simply.

He had given her a scornful look. "That's because you've already got everything. You're John Mitchell's daughter."

"Don't say it like that!" His words had cut harshly, deeply. "I'm me! Just me! I thought you liked me. I thought it didn't matter who I was," she said with despair. "It doesn't matter to me who you are!"

"Don't get mad."

"I hate you, Reese Sheridan!"

Then he grasped her by the shoulders with his thin, brown hands, and without warning he leaned toward her. The kiss had been brash, intense, fiery. It had subdued and frightened them both.

"I like you, Corliss," he said. "I like you a lot. Someday, you're going to belong to me."

From then on, it had been different. They never spoke of the future singly, but always as it would be for the two of them. The love grew. It endured. Through the teens, even into college days and separation, when she was sent to an exclusive

6

girls' college upstate and he struggled through a state college, working impossibly long hours to earn his tuition and studying as if a demon were about to consume him.

It was not something her parents had accepted wholeheartedly. The riverfront did not produce elite people. But gradually, the Mitchells came to understand that nothing could drive a wedge between them. They would not be separated, and wisely, her parents had stopped trying. They had even befriended Reese, although he couldn't quite accept the idea himself.

She had wanted to be married as soon as they graduated. Reese hadn't agreed.

"Everything has to be right, Corliss. Perfect. I'm going to have a good job, money, a home. And I don't want your father to make it easy for me. I have to do it on my own."

"I don't care about all those things, Reese. Just you. I don't want to wait!"

There were times when he nearly weakened. Times when he held her close and kissed her so hungrily that it was a wrench to part even for an hour. Times when she clung shamelessly to him and thought she could wait no longer. But he always broke away with a shake of his head.

"Not yet, Corliss. Be patient. It's not easy for me, either."

She knew it was pointless to try and persuade him, to change him. Down deep, Reese was still that determined, angry boy who had kissed her so ardently that day long ago at the mill. Eager, hungry, determined. But stubborn too and at times shortsighted. And unpredictable!

Corliss drew back the curtains in her room and saw the sky was showing pink. Dawn. But still several hours until time to meet Reese.

She dressed in comfortable clothes, giving in to her restlessness, and quietly left the house. Birds were stirring. The woods were never more enchanting than now. Trees were everywhere, growing with abandon, flinging branches skyward, seeking the morning sun. Inviting paths wound in and around them. There were squirrels, an occasional fox and an elusive hoot owl that she heard every night from her window.

Roberts Mill wasn't far. A short fifteen-minute hike. She found her way, taking a familiar path, feeling the sun growing warm on her brown hair, and she walked swiftly, using a stride that everyone referred to as the Bradford walk. She had inherited her mother's long legs and the slim body all Bradford women had.

"You're your mother's daughter," Father always told her. "Through and through."

"I'm glad," she always answered.

"Sometimes it makes my heart ache just looking at you."

But she didn't want to think of that now. Mother had been dead more than a year. But there were times when it seemed she should hear her voice or find her in the next room. For Father, it was even more lonely without her.

The mill came into view at last. A mist was rising from the green pool. The huge old wheel was moss-covered and broken, but still majestic. Everything had a look of age, a bit of yesterday caught and held as if in a camera slide. Shingles were silver with weather, a jagged windowpane was an ugly gash, and the stone walls were crumbling. But she loved the place. It would always be special.

Yesterday, at the lab, where she and Elizabeth Lane were working feverishly to finish the day's reports, the phone had rung. Elizabeth answered.

"It's for you, Corliss. Reese."

It gave her a start. Reese never phoned her at work unless it was very important or urgent.

"Hello," she said.

"Hello, darling," he said. His voice was singing. "Meet me at the mill. As soon as you can."

"The mill?" She laughed. "But why? I can't leave the lab until five, you know that."

"Hang the lab! Just once, get your nose out of a test tube and get yourself to the mill!"

"What's happened?"

"I'll tell you when I see you. Twenty

10

minutes."

"Thirty. It will surely take me thirty if I leave this instant —"

"Just be there!"

He hung up. She held the receiver for a moment, stunned.

"Something wrong?" Elizabeth asked.

"I don't know. Would you finish my report for me?"

Corliss left the lab five minutes later. She drove like the wind, just as she always went running when Reese beckoned. It seemed to take forever to get through the city traffic and out to the open highways. The road to Willow Woods was a winding one. The lane back to the mill was narrow and scarred with old ruts, but she skimmed over it as fast as she could. She brought her car to a halt in a cloud of dust and climbed out.

"Corliss!" He was there, waiting. She lifted an arm in greeting. He came to meet her, walking swiftly, and when she saw the look in his dark green eyes, she knew it was not an ordinary day for him. "I thought you'd never come."

He opened his arms and she went into them, like a little child lost and home again.

"But I set a record," she laughed. "Nineteen minutes."

He pushed her back in his arms so that she could see the hard slope of his jaw, the thick black hair, the dark brows and the firm lips. His teeth were white and straight and made him seem more handsome than he really was.

"Tell me. This instant!" she said.

"Burr's put me in charge of the Dumont acquisition. It's my baby! Do you know what that means?"

She laughed and took his face between her hands. "Oh, darling, what great news! You've talked of nothing else for the last few weeks!"

"I'm on my way, Corliss. No one will stop me now. No one! We're getting married! Tomorrow!"

She was so stunned that for a moment she couldn't speak. "I can't believe it! Do you really mean it?"

"We'll drive across the state line to

Brightwell. No waiting period there. We'll get the license, find a J.P. and be married. As simple as that!''

"Hold me tight, Reese. My head's spinning so. Hold me —''

She was crushed in his arms, smothered with a love that dispelled all good sense and erased the barest flash of disappointment. She had always pictured her wedding day at the Willow Woods church, a quaint, country chapel with stained glass windows and a tall spire. She had designed her bridal gown in her mind a dozen times. She had imagined what it would be like going down the aisle on her father's arm. But in the next moment, she let those things go. The important thing was the time had come at last.

"Is it true? Is it really going to happen?'' she asked.

"Yes, darling. It's true.''

There in the shadows of the old mill, where he had once kissed her as a brash young boy, he kissed her again, and as before, changed the road of her life.

"What about your father?'' he asked.

"He won't like this."

"No. But I'll handle him."

"It has to be my way. You understand?"

She pressed her cheek deeper into Reese's shoulder. "Yes. I understand."

"It's not going to be easy. Be sure about this, Corliss."

"I am sure, Reese. I love you. That's all that matters."

"Tomorrow," he murmured. "Tomorrow, darling."

Now tomorrow had come. She hadn't slept. She was teeming with excitement. But on the other hand, there was a tinge of guilt. Father would be so displeased about the elopement. He had never truly recovered from the shock of Mother's death. Then too, there was a bad feeling between him and Reese's boss, Burr Kaldner. They were business competitors now. Her father headed Mitchell Electronics and had enjoyed an open field until Burr Kaldner came riding in roughshod, hewing out a place for himself. The fact that Reese had gone to work for Burr was a constant thorn in Father's side.

Corliss took a deep breath. She would have willed it otherwise, but it was something they all had to live with. She could not give up Reese. Not for anyone or anything. But Father – she closed her eyes for a moment. He would be terribly upset! She thought about Drew Fielding. Drew had worked as company attorney for Mitchell Electronics for ten years. Father trusted and relied on him. Drew, in many ways, was like a son to him. To Corliss, Drew had been the rough-and-tumble older brother she'd never had.

With that thought in mind, she decided she must see Drew. This morning. There was time if she went now.

She took one last, loving look at Roberts Mill and noticed that the tall grass around it had been trampled down. Children had been playing here no doubt, just as she and Reese had in the past.

She hurried toward a path that would lead her to Drew's house. She took a shortcut to reach it and came to a startled halt. Someone else was here!

For a moment or two, real fright swept over her. There had been talk lately of prowlers in the woods and petty thefts. One neighbor had come home late at night to find the house ransacked. Since then, all of them had been more careful about locking doors.

Was that someone disappearing into the trees? Could it have been Mrs. Petrie, Drew's housekeeper, scurrying away so furtively? Oh, it couldn't have been Mrs. Petrie! Still —

I'm seeing things, she thought. I'm just so keyed up, I'm imagining things!

Then, dismissing the whole idea with a laugh, because this was a day that couldn't be spoiled, she hurried toward Drew's house, suddenly very eager to see him.

II

Willow Woods was ten miles from Sea-bourne and more populous, although it still had a feeling of isolation, of being a world unto itself. The houses were widely spaced, hidden, and no one bothered anyone else. It was a cardinal rule that one went calling only by invitation.

Except for Drew's house, she thought with a smile.

She had the run of his place. She went there whenever she pleased. Mrs. Petrie was never surprised to find her curled up in Drew's huge, comfortable chair with one of his books or romping on the terrace with his dog, Fuzz, or lying in wait for Drew by the gate.

Sun slanted through the trees. A mourning dove cried his lonely cry. For a moment she thought she saw the large brown eyes of a deer and then wasn't sure.

This morning she couldn't even trust her eyesight. First she had imagined she had seen Mrs. Petrie slipping away like a thief. Then a deer. But the deer did have the run of the woods and were often seen.

One last turn and she saw Drew's house. It was low, hugging the earth, made of native stone. The slate shingles were glistening with morning dew. The house was surrounded by a white picket fence and a gate that swung on oiled hinges. Everything about it was solid and cozy. Comfortable. Like Drew himself.

She was startled to see Mrs. Petrie. She was bringing out a bowl of bread and milk for Fuzz. Then surely Corliss hadn't seen her earlier slipping away from the mill. Still, Mrs. Petrie normally wore house slippers, in and out of the house – one of her many idiosyncrasies. Yet today, she wore stout, laced shoes and they were damp and stained, as if she had been walking through tall grass on this dewy morning!

"Hello, Corliss. You're out early."

"Yes." Corliss nodded. "Is Drew up?

And where's Fuzz? He always comes to meet me."

Mrs. Petrie gave her a smile that showed a broken front tooth. It gave her a pixie look. There were assorted tales about Mrs. Petrie. Corliss wasn't sure she believed any of them. Except that she had three grown sons. None of them were around Seabourne or Willow Woods anymore, and just as well. One of them, Ben, had been especially wild and always in some kind of trouble.

"Drew never was one to stay in bed past the crack of dawn. He's gone blackberrying," Mrs. Petrie replied.

"Blackberrying!" Corliss said with surprise.

"On the west ridge, if you want to find him."

Corliss knew where the blackberry patch was. She used to help Drew pick the berries. But the last time she'd gone to the patch had been several summers ago. Other things always got in the way lately, it seemed.

The blackberry patch wasn't far from

19

the house. Every year Drew went there, returning with thorn scratches on his long arms, sunburned and hot, but laden with succulent, juicy fruit.

She saw him at last, pail over his arm.

"Hi!" she called him.

He looked up, startled. Fuzz was leaping toward her and she gave him a quick hug, digging her fingers into his thick fur.

"What's wrong?" Drew asked. "Why are you here at this time of day? It isn't John, is it?"

"Father's fine. Still in bed when I left." She dipped her hand into his pail and helped herself to some of the berries. "Mm. Good! They're very sweet this year, aren't they?"

"They could have used more rain. I'm sure you didn't come here just to help me pick berries."

"Why not? Haven't done this in a long time," she said, flashing him a smile.

Drew eyed her. "You're up to something, Corliss. I know that look."

She laughed. Oh, she wanted to tell him! She wanted to tell the world. But they had agreed. It would be a secret. No one would know. Not until it was done!

"I can only stay a few minutes," she said. "But I'll help pick while I'm here."

She began plucking the berries, dropping them into Drew's pail. She saw the thick, rich brown of his hair with its glint of gray, already taking on a reddish tint from the sun. The breeze had rumpled him and she liked him best like this. He tolerated the city and the business suits he wore to the office. But he loved to loaf casually here at home, to roam the woods or read in his den.

"Drew—"

"Hmm?"

"Is there any more news about the prowler?"

Drew shook his head. "No. Why do you ask?"

She frowned, wondering if she should tell him about Mrs. Petrie. She didn't know that Mrs. Petrie had done anything wrong. Perhaps, like herself, she had merely been restless this morning and had gone for a walk.

"What do you know about Mrs. Petrie? Really, I mean?"

Drew gave her a tolerant smile. "Mrs. Petrie is odd, perhaps. Eccentric, if you will. But she does her work well. She's a good cook. Looks after all my wants. She's not too communicative, but—"

"Do you believe all the stories about her?"

"Of course not! People like to gossip, that's all. She had some bad luck with her kids. Ben, in particular. And her husband, before he died, was the town handyman — who would rather sleep in the sun than work. Under the circumstances, the poor woman has done well by herself."

"Still—"

Drew laughed. "I know you didn't come here just to gossip about Mrs. Petrie."

"I thought I saw her around the old mill this morning, slipping away like a shadow. Now why would she be there?"

Drew pulled his heavy brows together. "Why would you?"

"Just out for an early walk. You know

I love the old mill. Now about Mrs. Petrie—"

Drew frowned. "Until she does something terrible, like burn the house down, I intend to keep her!"

"You don't have to get peevish!"

"Sometimes, Corliss, you make no sense at all. Here you are, picking berries, worrying about my housekeeper, when all the time you're hatching some kind of scheme. It's written all over you."

She plunked a handful of berries into the pail, laughing. "Isn't this enough? Can't we quit now?"

"I suppose so. It's getting hot, anyway."

He whistled for Fuzz and they tramped out of the meadows, leaving the blackberry bushes to the sun. Even with her long legs, she had to hurry to keep up with him.

At the house, Drew gave the pail of berries to Mrs. Petrie. "Bring us a couple of bowls, will you?" he asked. "Don't be stingy with the cream. We'll be in the den."

Ah, the den! Her favorite place of all

favorite places! It was a large room and had a fragrance all its own. Partly of the woods, partly of Drew's pipe tobacco, mostly of books, paper, ink, a very delicious fragrance, one she found herself sniffing almost eagerly.

It was cool in the den, a relief after the hot sun of the berry patch. Sliding doors opened out to a brick-floored terrace and comfortable lawn chairs. The walls were lined with bookshelves. A large, rather shabby desk commanded the room like a captain his ship. The fireplace was smoke-stained, huge, and she couldn't begin to remember the times she had sat before its roaring flames, content there as she was never content anywhere else, unless it was when she was with Reese.

Corliss sank into her favorite chair. Drew reached up to a shelf and plucked down a book. He tossed it into her lap.

"Read that," he said.

She laughed. "Drew Fielding, do you know how many times you've pulled books down from those shelves and commanded me to read them?"

He took a pipe from the clutter on the desk and filled it with tobacco. "It got you through college, didn't it? And all those extra courses so that you got the lab technician job at the Gilman Laboratories you wanted."

"Yes," she said and she felt serious for a moment. "You helped me more than I can ever repay you."

He lifted his brows at that. "Why the bouquet of flowers all of a sudden?"

She laughed. "Oh, I don't know. I'm in a mellow mood perhaps, and I do owe you a great deal, Drew. You were always there when I needed you."

"So?" he nodded. "That's why you've come. You've gotten yourself in some kind of a jam. You need a good lawyer. What did you do? Wreck your car? Get a traffic ticket?"

"Nothing like that!"

He puffed at his pipe, and it was plain that he was growing more curious by the minute about her unexpected, early morning visit. "What, then?"

"Nothing," she insisted. "Not like you

mean. I know I've been a real headache in the past."

"Headache!" he exclaimed. "Sometimes, I had to threaten to turn you over my knee, and there you were, a college coed –"

"Was I so awful?"

He pointed the stem of his pipe at her. "When the phone rang at three in the morning, I always knew it would be you. You were scared you were going to flunk a test. Or there was something wrong with your car. Or you needed money. Or you were angry with Reese. Or your parents. I can recall a time or two when you threatened to leave college and come home for good."

She laughed. "Drew, was I ever that young and impossible?"

"It seems only yesterday, Corliss."

A wave of nostalgia swept over her heart, tugging at it, and she found herself shivering on the brink, afraid to take the leap across the chasm of yesterday into today and tomorrow, and yet knowing that it was inevitable that she would.

Mrs. Petrie shuffled into the room. She was wearing her house slippers now. The wet, stained shoes were gone. Again, Corliss wondered about it.

"Here you are, dearie," Mrs. Petrie said. "All sweetened and creamed."

"Thank you," said Drew, nodding.

In a few moments, Mrs. Petrie had gone, humming a song under her breath. Drew handed Corliss a bowl of the berries. "Breakfast fit for a king," he said.

They ate the berries, devouring them hungrily until they were exchanging purple-stained smiles. Then Drew put their bowls aside with a meaningful gesture, and she knew he was about to demand answers.

"Now," he said. "Let's get down to the crux of the matter."

She took a deep breath. There was one thing she could do for Father to make the news of her elopement easier. "Come to dinner tonight," she said.

"Dinner?"

"Yes. Please."

He was puzzled. He relighted his pipe

and eyed her above the blaze of his match. "Is that all? Come to dinner?"

"Yes."

"All right. I'll come."

Corliss got quickly to her feet. Time was slipping away. She must get back. "I'll tell Martha to expect you."

When she phoned Father tonight with the news, he was bound to be upset and angry, unreasonable. But Drew could always calm him. He could talk sense to Father. It never occurred to her that Drew would ever take sides against her. He never had.

She moved to the glass doors. It came to her rather abruptly that after today, she wouldn't be coming here like this. Things would be different. For one thing, Reese didn't like Drew. She couldn't imagine why, but he didn't. How could anyone not like Drew?

This house and Drew had been part of her life ever since she had been an impressionable fifteen-year-old girl. But it was time to put away childish things. Time to break with the past and start a new life.

28

She found her eyes stinging with tears. She rushed back to Drew and reached up to put her arms around his neck and leave a feathery kiss across his suntanned cheek. Drew stiffened with surprise.

"What was that for?" he asked gruffly.

"For nothing. Just nothing."

Then she hurried out the door, through the gate, and up the path toward home. Toward the growing day. Toward Reese.

III

The sun was putting golden outlines on everything, crushing the scent from the pines and opening the wildflowers. There would be time for breakfast with her father before she changed and went to the lab to meet Reese.

The good smell of fresh coffee greeted her as she entered the house. Martha had breakfast ready and waiting. Her father was already at the table.

"Good morning, Father," Corliss said cheerfully.

"You're in a very bright mood. Where were you? I waited."

"Picking berries with Drew. It's a positively gorgeous day!"

Her father was a tall, slender man with white hair neatly combed. He had a certain regal bearing about him. His eyes were a keen blue, but they softened when he looked at her.

"By the way, I invited Drew to dinner tonight," she said.

"Good! I always enjoy his company. If we're lucky, we might have something important to celebrate."

She looked up. "Celebrate?"

"A business deal. One we've been working on for weeks. We may close it today. But I don't want to talk about it. It might jinx it, you know. Tell me about the lab. And Doctor Gilman. And Elizabeth. How's Elizabeth?"

"Elizabeth is fine. Doctor Gilman is a wonder. Really, a wonder. Someday, I predict he'll be famous. Like Doctor Salk or Alexander Fleming."

"And you, my dear? What about you?" Father asked.

She laughed and brushed back a lock of brown hair. "I'm only a lab technician, Father."

"You're being modest. I know first-hand what a real contribution you're making there. I'm proud of you."

"You're sweet, Father. Do you know

that?"

He laughed. "Doctor Gilman told me himself that you are the most efficient technician he's ever had work for him. You and Elizabeth make a great team."

She measured two spoonfuls of sugar into her coffee and gave it one stir. "Sometimes it frightens me, Father. We do all the lab reports and tests for all the doctors within a radius of twenty-five miles of Seabourne. We know the general health of nearly everyone. Sometimes –"

Father reached out and patted her hand. "Think of all the good news you have for people, in comparison to the bad."

"You're right, of course. I love the lab. It's another world. Part of me belongs there."

"And the other part?" Father asked with a slight frown crossing his face.

"It belongs to Reese Sheridan."

They looked at each other. She saw the old disapproval come to the surface of his blue eyes, and then quickly it bobbed away. It was on the tip of her tongue to tell him of her plans. There would never be a better time. But she couldn't.

The moment passed. Her father finished his breakfast and pushed back from the table. "I had a surprising phone call yesterday," he said. "From the Widow Huffman."

Corliss blinked. "Madeline Huffman phoned you? Why? Don't tell me she's finally decided to be neighborly. And why do you call her Widow Huffman? She's barely in her thirties. You make her sound like a woman who has been years and years without a husband."

Father smiled. "Just habit. A throwback to the old days. A widow is a widow, after all. She wants to see me. I expect she'll be dropping by in a day or two."

"I can't imagine why."

"Nor can I. Strange woman. Quite lovely, you know. But why she decided to settle in Willow Woods, no one seems to know."

"Maybe she's hiding from someone," Corliss said. "Or she's the victim of an unhappy love affair. Maybe she's really a spy in disguise. But what would she be spying on in sleepy little Willow Woods?"

Father made a face. "You always had the wildest imagination, Corliss. Whatever she's doing here is none of our affair."

"I suppose not."

"Now, I must be getting ready for the office."

"When are you going to retire? You keep promising—"

He turned back to her. "It's so empty here now. How could I endure it for twenty-four hours out of every day?"

She was sorry she had mentioned it, for it only recalled her mother to him. Losing her had taken such a deep, personal toll. It had robbed some of the brightness from his eyes and brought a slight stoop to his shoulders. She was reminded that he was not young anymore, and that tonight when she phoned, it would be another blow. She only hoped and prayed that Drew could make it easier for him.

John Mitchell was a proud man, first

and foremost. He had built Mitchell Electronics into a very profitable and lucrative business. The firm manufactured a variety of electrical equipment. Generally, it had defense contracts, and sometimes, it did special work – right now it was building a piece of lab test equipment which Paul Gilman had spent years designing.

In her room, Corliss changed, brushed her brown-blonde hair until it shone like the sun itself, and saw that her blue eyes glowed with excitement. It was odd that neither her father nor Martha had noticed.

At last, she called goodbye and stepped out into the growing day. As she closed the door behind her, she paused for a moment. For all of her twenty-five years she had lived here. She and Reese had not discussed where they would begin their new life together.

The road to Seabourne wound through the meadows and hills of Willow Woods and eventually out to the busy highway. The sun was climbing fast now, and the dew had already burned off. As she drove past the snug little house where Madeline Huffman lived, she spotted Drew's car in the driveway. For a moment, her own car swerved with surprise. That was the third time she had known Drew to be there.

Drew wasn't the type that practiced the good neighbor policy literally. Yet Madeline Huffman was an attractive woman. Perhaps it was true that men like a bit of mystery. As far as Corliss knew, Drew had never been seriously involved with any woman since he came to Seabourne and Willow Woods. She had wondered about that from time to time. But somehow, it was upsetting to think he might be interested in Madeline Huffman.

She drove on, putting it out of her mind, for there was really only room for Reese there. Reese! Her beloved Reese! At long last, they were to be married!

She reached the lab and hurried inside. There was still more than an hour before Reese would be coming for her. She must check several things with Elizabeth and advise Paul Gilman that she would be away for a few days.

She went to find Paul. He was always at the lab early. He spent unbelievably long hours there. Paul was before his microscope, peering intently into it, a batch of slides at one elbow and a pad of paper at the other.

"Hi," he said. "You're early."

"Something interesting?" she asked.

He pushed back from the microscope, a pale man in his late forties with prematurely gray hair. But he had a nice smile and quiet eyes.

"Not yet. But I keep hoping."

"You never give up, do you, Paul."

"No. Coffee? I just made a fresh pot."

She shook her head. "Paul, I know this is short notice, but I'm going to be away for a few days."

Paul poured his coffee and sipped it for a moment. "Something urgent?"

"Yes."

"I see. Well, we'll manage. Don't worry about it. I won't ask questions. I sense it's personal."

"Very personal."

"Okay. Just brief Elizabeth on your work. I checked the report you did yesterday, and I agree. The tests seem inconclusive. Better run another series. Doctor Monroe phoned earlier. He needs some skin tissue examined immediately. His office nurse will bring the slides."

It was an effort to concentrate on Paul's instructions. Then at last, everything was in order. Elizabeth still had not arrived and Corliss wasn't certain she could keep her secret once Elizabeth came. She paced about the lab, a bright and shining room she loved, waiting for the sound of Elizabeth's steps coming down the hall.

"Hi!"

Elizabeth came into the room, a tall, pretty woman with a sweet face and gentle eyes.

"Oh, I thought you'd never come!" Corliss said.

"Hey, what's up?" Elizabeth asked with a low laugh. "You're positively glowing!"

Corliss laughed and reached out to grasp Elizabeth's cool hands. "Oh, I can't keep it. Not from you, Elizabeth. Reese and I are going to be married. Today. At Brightwell."

"You're eloping!"

"Yes. We'll find a justice of the peace and—"

Elizabeth's brown eyes flickered. "No wedding in the Willow Woods church?"

"No."

"But you so wanted—"

"I want to marry Reese. That's all that's important."

Elizabeth leaned toward her to give her a quick kiss. "I'm happy for you. So happy! I know how much you love Reese. I think it's wonderful—"

Then she broke off, and for a moment, there was an air of sadness about her. "You're very lucky, Corliss."

"You never hear from Alex anymore, do you?"

Elizabeth shook her head. "You know I don't."

"I wish—"

"I've forgotten him," Elizabeth said firmly.

But Corliss knew she hadn't. Alex Ward had left his mark on Elizabeth. Sweet, trusting, innocent Elizabeth had been taken in by Alex's smooth ways. Alex never played for keeps. But Elizabeth had been too blindly in love with him to realize that.

Corliss looked at her watch for the sixth time in five minutes. Reese would be coming any minute now. She paced the floor impatiently. Then, at last, she caught sight of him from the window, and he waved to her.

"He's here! I'm going now, Elizabeth."

"Good luck! Take care."

Corliss rushed out of the lab to Reese's car. He leaped out and drew her close for a moment. "Is it really happening, Reese?" she asked. "Am I dreaming?"

"It's no dream this time!"

Elizabeth was watching from the window. They waved to her.

"Reese, I told her," Corliss said. "I

just couldn't keep it."

"It's all right." Reese smiled. "Let's be on our way."

They joined the morning traffic. As they reached the open highway, Corliss saw that the perfect day was still holding. There wasn't a cloud in the sky. For the next two hours, they talked of their plans, where they would live temporarily, the house they might buy later, where they would go for a very brief honeymoon.

They reached Brightwell, purchased their license, and found their way to the office of the justice of the peace.

The J.P. was an old man with a bald head and blue eyes. He studied the license and lifted his gaze to Corliss.

"Are you Corliss Mitchell?"

"Yes."

"I have a message for you."

He handed her a slip of paper. But no one knew they were coming here! No one but Elizabeth. She smiled. A message of congratulations probably. It was something Elizabeth would do.

But the message was not what she

expected. It was a phone number. She was to call it immediately. The number was that of her father's office. A tremor went along her arms. Something was wrong. Very wrong!

IV

"Darling, what is it?" Reese asked. "You've gone as pale as a ghost."

"It's Father's office."

Reese's lips made a firm line.

"How did he find out we were here? He wants to stop us, that's all!"

"I don't think it's that. Only Elizabeth knew we were coming. She wouldn't have told anyone unless it was a real emergency. I must phone, Reese."

It seemed to take hours to get the call through. Then she heard Drew's voice on the other end of the line.

"Corliss!" he said. "Where are you? Elizabeth said you'd phone right back. I've been waiting for your call."

"I just now got your message. What is it?"

There was a moment of silence over the line. Then Drew's voice was deep and quiet. "It's your father, Corliss. I'm afraid he's had a stroke."

Corliss gripped the phone tightly. For a moment, a terrible ringing started up in her ears.

"How serious?"

"It's possible that it's very serious. Get to the hospital as quickly as you can. I'll meet you there. Are you at the lab?"

"I'm in Brightwell."

"Across the state line? What are you doing there?"

"Never mind. I'll come. As soon as I can."

She hung up. Reese's hands gripped her arm tightly, and his green eyes were dark with questions. She explained in an uneven voice what had happened.

"Reese, I have to get back. Right away."

"But we're going to be married! I've waited so long for this day. I'm not going to let it slip out of my hands now!"

She shook her head. "I want this as much as you. But how can I stay? I have to go back, Reese. Oh, Reese – hold me – tell me that this isn't happening. How could everything go wrong now?''

She leaned her head on his shoulder, the world spinning out of control, her heart torn in two directions.

"It's not fair!" Reese said angrily. "It's not fair!"

Tears stung her eyes. They ran down her cheeks, and Reese's face softened when he saw them. He took a deep, resigned breath. He looked whipped, defeated. He rubbed away her tears with his fingers.

"We'll go. Right away. The license will keep. But we'll come back, Corliss. Soon. Promise me that."

"Yes. Soon."

It was a silent, nightmare ride back to Seabourne. Reese seldom took his eyes from the road, and she could feel his disappointment like a heavy mist around her face. Today was to have been such a happy day. Now it had come to this.

She ached with despair, but not only for Reese and herself, but for her father. How ill was he? Drew wasn't an alarmist. He had said it might be serious, and she knew that Drew had told her the truth.

She wished Reese would drive faster. It seemed the car was only inching along. Her head was aching. She felt chilled. "I just don't know what could have happened. At breakfast, Father was fine. Bright and alert."

"He'll be all right," Reese said confidently. "I'm sorry if back there I seemed – well – selfish. I'm worried about your father too, Corliss."

"I know. I understand. Poor Reese."

"Poor both of us," he murmured.

At last, after what seemed an eternity, they reached Seabourne, drove straight to the hospital, and hurried inside.

"I'll wait for you in the lobby, darling," Reese said. "I wouldn't want to upset your father."

"But I need you, Reese! Please, I'm so frightened."

He shook his head. "I'm thinking of your father now," Reese said.

"But why would seeing you upset him?" she asked.

He leaned down and brushed his lips across her cheek. "Run along. I'll wait here."

He put her on the elevator, and she was swept upward to the third floor, her heart in her mouth, her worst fears coming to the surface. She dreaded this. She feared it. Father was not young anymore –

When she stepped off the elevator, she was relieved to see Drew pacing up and down the corridor. "Drew –"

He came to her swiftly with his long stride, his big face worried, his brown hair rumpled. "What took so long?"

"I came as quickly as I could. How is he? Drew, tell me the truth –"

"He wants to see you. His speech has been affected, but that may be a temporary thing. Don't let it throw you."

"But what happened?"

A wave of remorse passed over Drew's face. "I'm afraid I'm to blame."

"You!" she exclaimed.

"I had to give him some bad news today. You didn't know. No one knew. But we were trying to acquire the Dumont plant."

She froze, her head spinning. The Dumont acquisition! The business transaction that had prompted Reese to elope with her had cost her father a stroke? She felt the blood drain out of her face.

"It was important to us, Corliss. Very important. Burr Kaldner beat us to it. I suppose you know that Reese is to handle the acquisition."

"And because of this, Father—"

Drew nodded soberly. "Yes, I really think that's what caused it."

"Oh, no. No!"

Drew put a hand on her shoulder. "Easy now. Keep your chin up. Just remember your father's ill, and he wants to see you."

They paused outside a closed door. She ran her shaking fingers over her forehead. "I don't think I can go in, Drew."

He put his arm around her shoulder. "You must. Come along. I'll be right beside you."

She stepped into the room, grateful to Drew for his support and kindness. She supposed the room was an ordinary hospital room. She didn't know. She could see only her father's long frame on the bed. His face seemed so white. But his eyes were open, searching. He saw her.

"I'm here, Father. I'm here."

She took his hand. She wasn't sure, but she thought he tried to smile. She kept talking to him, quietly, reassuring him. He gripped her hand a little tighter. Then he seemed to breathe more deeply, and in a short while he had fallen asleep.

"They gave him a shot just before you came," Drew explained. "He'll sleep for some time now. Come along."

He tugged her out of the room, and it was then the impact of all that had happened hit her. It was almost like a physical blow that sickened her. She covered her face with her hands and began to sob. Drew put his arm around her, and she clung to him, crying for her father, but crying for Reese too, and herself.

When would the sun ever shine as brightly again as it had today for a few hours? When?

It was late. Elizabeth had come to the house anxious for news, doing her best to cheer Corliss.

"He'll be all right," Elizabeth had said. "I just know he will. Your father has so much strength and courage."

Corliss nodded. "Yes, I keep remembering that."

There had been other phone calls from neighbors who had heard about the stroke. A few of her father's business acquaintances also phoned.

Then at last, due to the lateness of the hour, the phone had stopped ringing. Martha, eyes reddened from worried, faithful tears, had made coffee and left the tray. Reese stood quietly looking out the terrace doors into the night, hands in his pockets, his shoulders rigid.

"You knew what must have happened," Corliss said. "That's why you didn't want to see Father at the hospital."

"Yes. I'd heard your father was trying to buy the Dumont plant as well as us."

"And it made no difference!"

Reese gave her a quick, dark look. "Not to Burr. Business is business with Burr."

"What about you?"

Reese set his jaw. He murmured something angrily to himself. He came to stand before her. "It was business! My job. What else was I to do? It's a heck of a spot for me to be in, Corliss. I admire your father. You know that! Do you think I set out deliberately to make him ill?"

He was upset and angry and perhaps she wasn't being fair. He came to sit down beside her, and he pulled her close. He kissed her forehead, her eyes, her lips.

"Darling, darling, we have each other. Nothing can change that. No matter what happens. We have each other."

"Oh, Reese, what if he doesn't get well—"

He soothed her and consoled her until she began to get a hold on herself again.

"This will work out. Believe me, Corliss, it will."

"But how? With my father on one side of the fence and you on the other and me somewhere in the middle?''

''But what can I do? Give up my job, my career? Do you want that?''

''Of course not!''

''I can go places fast with Burr Kaldner, Corliss. I know it, and you know it, whether you want to admit it or not!''

''I'm not asking you to give up your work.''

''Then what are you asking?''

''I don't know. To make a miracle perhaps. To erase today so we can start it all over again.''

''Tomorrow things will look brighter. Believe me, they will. Besides, your father's a fair man. He'll understand. He won't hold the Dumont deal against me.''

But Reese didn't really believe that and neither did she. Her father had a stubborn streak in him. He was, after all, only human. For a man like John Mitchell, having his daughter engaged to a man who worked for Burr Kaldner was bad enough, but to add to it the fact that they had stolen away a choice business plum – she shook her head. No, it wasn't going to be so simple.

"I'll go now. Try to get some rest," Reese said. "I'll phone you tomorrow."

She walked with him to the door. There, he held her close for a moment and kissed her lightly. Then he was gone. She listened to the sound of his car driving away. The silence came down on Willow Woods, and the house seemed very large and empty. She carefully locked the door, mindful of the prowler.

She went to bed. But not to sleep. How could she sleep after all that had happened?

The next morning, she left the house early. She stopped at the hospital and looked in on her father, but he was still sleeping.

"He had a good night, Miss Mitchell," the nurse told her.

"Will you please tell him I stopped by?"

"Yes, of course. The minute he's awake."

There was nothing to do but go to the lab. Thank God for the lab! For the routine of hard work. For the hours of bending over a microscope until her shoulders cramped and her neck ached.

Elizabeth was already there.

"Any news?" she asked.

"He had a good night. I stopped by the hospital."

"I knew it! I know it's not going to be too serious."

"Thanks for the encouraging words. I needed them. It was a long night. I couldn't sleep."

"You need some coffee. Paul put on a fresh pot. I'll get you a cup."

"Coffee?" she asked wearily. "I suppose it will help clear my head. I just want to work, Elizabeth. Hard. I don't want a minute to think of anything else."

"Sometimes I wish I hadn't gotten in touch with you at Brightwell yesterday. But when Drew phoned, it sounded so serious."

"You did the right thing."

"But your elopement, all your plans – Reese – what will happen now?"

"Everything just has to wait. It seems

that's all Reese and I have done. Wait.''

Corliss took a deep breath. There was no use crying over spilled milk. It was done. It couldn't be helped. All she could do now was take one day at a time.

For the next few days, Corliss worked harder at the lab than she ever had before. Never before had she run through so many tests or typed so many reports. She even found time to help Paul with some of his research experiments. She visited the hospital three times a day – every morning when she drove in from Willow Woods, every lunch hour she snatched a few minutes to spend with her father, and every evening she stayed until visiting hours were over.

The doctor gave her good news. The stroke had not been as serious as they had first thought. Her father made rapid improvements. His speech cleared, and he was alert. But there was a general weakness on his left side that would make it difficult for him to walk without some kind of assistance.

He never once mentioned Reese, nor

did she. Or the Dumont affair. But it seemed to be in the room with them every time she visited him.

Ten days later, Corliss drove her father home from the hospital. He sat quietly, a pale man who watched from the window and said almost nothing. By the time they had reached the house and found Martha and Samuel Worth waiting for them at the doorstep, Father seemed very tired.

"Welcome home, Mr. Mitchell," Martha said with a happy smile. "It's good to have you back. I've fixed a very special lunch for you. Would you like it on the terrace?"

"I'm not very hungry," Father said.

It took half an hour to get him comfortably settled in the living room. Drew phoned to welcome him home, and Corliss gave him a gift that had been left for him, a leather-bound edition of Thoreau.

"Thoreau!" Father murmured, pleased. "Who brought this?"

She took a deep breath. "Reese."

He raised his head to look at her, and a blankness came to his eyes. He put the book aside and did not open it.

"I see."

"Father—"

"I don't want to talk about Reese or Burr Kaldner!"

"I can understand why you're angry with Burr, but Reese—"

"Reese is his little puppy dog, following around behind him, like—like—"

He clamped his lips shut and turned his head away. She knew the subject was closed. At least for now. She ran a shaky hand across her forehead. At best, in the past, the relationship between her father and the man she loved had been touchy. Now it seemed impossible.

Somehow, some way, Corliss got through the next few days, driving herself at the lab, freezing a smile on her face when she went home at night, praying that her father's outlook would have changed. But she always found him the same.

Reese phoned her every morning at the lab. As often as they could, they met for lunch. Their first luncheon had been tense and uncomfortable.

"So, your father does blame me," Reese said tiredly.

"He's ill. Perhaps with time —"

"Time," Reese sighed. "What's so magic about time? What shall I do? What do you want me to do to make things right?"

She shook her head. "I don't know. The Dumont deal is finished."

"It's not just the Dumont deal. It's me. Reese Sheridan. Riverfront brat. Daring to put a foot in Willow Woods. It goes deeper than the Dumont affair. Don't you see that, Corliss?"

There was the old hunger and desire burning in his eyes. She remembered him when she had first seen him at the old mill, a stranger in an enchanted land, wanting it all for himself. She had understood him then and felt compassion and in time, love. She felt it now, only more deeply.

"It was always you who said there would be a time for us, Reese. We can't give up now. We can't!"

He stared at her and slowly began to relax. He nodded. "You're right. Just say

58

you think no less of me. That you still love me –"

She reached out to take his hand. "I love you, Reese. Nothing can ever change that."

He raised her hand to his lips and kissed her fingers, one at a time, holding them at last against his cheek. Then he smiled, and she knew that she could endure, that she could wait, that she could not give up hope.

She was surprised when Reese called late one Friday afternoon at the lab. He hadn't been able to meet her for lunch because of a business meeting. Now, his voice over the phone sounded cheerful and enthusiastic.

"Corliss, I want you to come to dinner with me tonight."

"I'd love to. But you know I can't."

There was a moment of silence. Then Reese's voice was firm and determined. "You haven't been out of the house since your father came home from the hospital. You need to get out. Besides, this is very important."

"What is it? Can't you tell me?"

He laughed. "No. Not now. Not on the phone. I'll come by for you at seven."

She hesitated a moment. There had to be a first time. Martha and Samuel Worth would be with Father, and Drew nearly always dropped by every evening. Father would not be alone or want for anything.

"I'll meet you in town, Reese. It would be better that way."

"All right. If you prefer. The Town House. Seven."

She hung up thoughtfully, wondering why Reese had been so jubilant. The Town House was not his favorite place. Why were they going there?

When she told her father she was going out for the evening, he studied her silently. He asked no questions, and she was relieved. But she saw the look of disapproval go across his pale face. Drew arrived for his usual visit before she left. It made it easier.

She drove to Seabourne and found Reese waiting for her. The Town House was plush and expensive. The head waiter nodded to them.

"This way, Mr. Sheridan."

They followed him, and Reese kept a firm hand on her elbow, almost as if he were afraid she'd run away. They stopped at a table already occupied, and in a flash, she saw Burr Kaldner and his daughter, Jennie. She gave Reese a quick, startled look.

"I hope we're not late, Burr," Reese said.

Reese's fingers dug into her elbow, a warning.

"Not at all, Reese," Burr said. "How are you, Miss Mitchell?"

V

Corliss was too startled to say anything for the moment. Why had Reese done this? There was no one in the world she wanted to see less than Burr Kaldner right now!

Reese applied still more pressure with his fingers on her elbow. She lifted her chin.

"Hello, Mr. Kaldner," she said. "Hello, Jennie."

Jennie was twenty or so, but somehow seemed younger. She gave Corliss a bright, sweet smile. Burr got to his feet and held her chair. Reese seemed completely at ease on the surface, but Corliss knew by the tense lines around his mouth that he was anything but relaxed. She tried to catch his eyes, but he avoided her gaze.

"I've already ordered for us," Burr

said. "Hope it will be satisfactory."

"It will be fine, I'm sure," Reese said quickly.

Burr was eyeing Corliss from under his shaggy brows. From an inside pocket he brought out a cigar, clipped it with a fancy little cutter, and lighted it, rolling it between his pudgy fingers.

"How is your father, Corliss?" Burr asked.

She steeled herself. All the angry, hurt, anxious words came rushing to her lips. But she conquered them and held them back. "He's as well as can be expected under the circumstances."

"I was sorry to hear about it," Burr said.

"Thank you."

"He's such a handsome gentleman," Jennie spoke up. "Do you know, he's stylish! He really is."

Reese laughed awkwardly. Burr smiled and then reached over to touch Jennie's silky blonde hair. "Don't mind my daughter, Corliss," Burr said. "She's like that, you know. Smitten with everything."

Jennie clasped her small hands on the tabletop. "I mean it! I really do mean it."

And she did. Even Corliss couldn't discount Jennie Kaldner's sincerity. Sometimes Corliss wondered how a roughcut man like Burr could have such a sweet, angelic daughter.

Burr was short and stocky with a large head set close to his beefy shoulders. He wore expensive clothes, but somehow, on him they looked untidy. His tie was never quite straight. The handkerchief in his pocket had been stuffed in hurriedly. A large diamond flashed on his little finger. It was hard to imagine how he had come to hold such position in Seabourne.

"You're a good sport, Corliss," Burr said with a slow smile. "Coming to our little victory party for the Dumont acquisition."

A coldness settled around her heart. She darted a look at Reese. He gave her a quick, tense smile.

"Corliss is a good sport, Burr. She knows what this has meant to us. To me," Reese said.

"Sorry we had to step on your father's toes, Corliss," Burr said slowly.

Corliss stared at him. He looked smug and confident. In that moment, she hated him.

"You know how it is. Business," he said smoothly. "Nothing personal, you understand. I'm a great admirer of your father."

"Oh, for goodness' sake," Jennie cut in. "Must we talk, talk, talk about business!"

Burr laughed. "Now, daughter, business people talk business, you know."

"I agree with Jennie," Corliss said quickly. "After hours, it's nice just to enjoy oneself, isn't it?"

Burr's dark eyes flashed. He looked at her steadily, and she met his gaze, chin up, her anger simmering just under the surface. Reese knew the signs. He changed the subject abruptly. "Ah, here comes our first course. Looks good. I'm hungry. Aren't you, Corliss?"

She didn't think she could eat any of the food. But she knew she must. Burr was watching every move she made, listening to her every word. He wanted to see some little crack show in her composure. He wanted to break her down. Inch by inch. Even though he was outwardly polite, charming, even kind, she didn't trust him.

Burr began to monopolize the conversation. He talked of his earlier days, and the struggle he'd had. His stories were blunt, a little coarse. Reese seemed to be drinking them in, encouraging them. Then suddenly, Burr leaned toward Corliss.

"I've come a long way, miss. I aim to go a lot farther."

"I'm sure you will," she said coolly. "You have a very good man working for you." She reached out to put a hand on Reese's sleeve. She needed to touch him. She had to make contact with reality, for surely all of this was happening in some kind of bad dream. How could Reese have put her through this? Was it so important to crawl to Burr Kaldner, to jump at his every command? Surely Reese didn't have some crazy idea of making friends of the two of them!

"I got plans for Reese, Corliss. Big plans," Burr said in a quiet voice. Burr pushed his plate back. He had not eaten much for a large man. He lighted another cigar. "When we've all finished, we'll go to the house for desert. I promised Jennie."

Corliss looked at Reese with a start. Couldn't he excuse them? Couldn't he sense that she wanted nothing more than to go home, to leave these people?

"I made it myself!" Jennie said shyly. "Something special. I'm a good cook. I really am."

"I'm sure whatever it is, it's delicious, Jennie," Reese said.

Corliss tried to send messages with her eyes to Reese, but he was ignoring her. He was bound that they would go. She was being dragged unwillingly into the enemy camp. What would her father say if he knew this was happening? She ached at the thought.

Soon they were leaving the Town House. Jennie was a small woman, almost tiny. A wisp of a thing. Corliss felt overly tall in her presence. There was a sweetness about Jennie. A sunniness. She was genuinely friendly. Naïve. It was impossible not to like the girl.

"Do you ride, Corliss?" Jennie asked.

"No."

"I do. I'm wild about horses. I want to buy one of my own, but Daddy keeps being mean about it! He says I'll just fall off and break my neck," Jennie said with a laugh.

They made their way to their cars. Somehow, Jennie ended up walking beside Reese. Corliss was only too well aware of what an attractive couple they made. The tall, older, handsome man with jet black hair, and the tiny, almost frail blonde girl with such adoration in her eyes. Corliss would have been blind not to have seen how Jennie kept watching Reese all evening, hanging on to every word.

They climbed into their cars, Jennie going with her father. Reese started the motor and followed Burr.

"How could you?" Corliss asked,

hands gripped tightly together.

Reese glanced at her. "I had to come tonight. Burr insisted I bring you."

"So he could gloat about the Dumont acquisition?"

"Don't be silly!" Reese said angrily.

"I'm not. But if you think that wasn't his entire purpose, you're blind, Reese!"

"It was important that I come. I work for the man, Corliss! Let's just leave your father out of this. What's he got to do with you and me, anyway? You've a right to your own life."

"I won't talk about it, Reese. Not here. Not now!"

Reese shot her an angry, dark look. "Someday soon, you may have to talk about it!"

Corliss turned away. More than anything, she just wanted to go home before this grew into a real quarrel.

"Burr's not as bad as you paint him," Reese said. "For my sake, be nice. The evening will soon be over."

"And what about Jennie?"

Reese turned his head to give her

a quick look.

"Does she always fawn over you so much?" Corliss asked.

Reese stared at her. "What are you implying?"

"That Jennie's sweet on you. Anyone can see it. She eats you up with those big blue eyes of hers!"

"Jennie is a sweet kid. A child, really. Immature for her age. She's been sick a lot. Now, let's leave her out of this!"

Corliss sighed. She rubbed her forehead with shaking fingers. She felt cold. "I'm sorry. I like the girl too. I'm being unreasonable, I suppose."

They reached the Kaldner house. It was a large, rambling place, expensive, built originally by a man named Tucker who at one time had owned a great deal of Seabourne. Since then, Tucker had died, the property had been hacked up in settling the estate, and Burr Kaldner had bought the house.

"We'll stay no longer than necessary," Reese said. "Now, promise me you'll be nice."

"I'll try."

They got out and went up to the brightly lighted doorway. A maid answered their ring. Then Burr was there, between them, taking their arms and leading them inside. The room was ornately furnished. There wasn't a piece there that wasn't expensive, perhaps specially made, but somehow it looked too much like a showplace. Corliss much preferred her own home or Drew's comfortable, cozy cottage.

Jennie came to take Corliss's hand. "Come along with me to the kitchen. You can help. The maid would do it, but I'd rather serve tonight, since I made it. It's a recipe I found in an old cookbook."

Jennie seemed almost childishly proud of her accomplishments. The dessert was light, fluffy, and appetizing. Jennie dished it up on chilled plates and filled Corliss's ears with all kinds of recipes as she worked.

"Do you cook, Corliss?"

Corliss laughed. "No. Only on the Bunsen burner."

Jennie gave her a bright, blue-eyed look. "You know, I envy you! What you do at the lab is very important, isn't it?"

"Yes."

"I guess I'm not smart enough for anything like that. Besides, Daddy won't let me go to college. He's always afraid I'll get sick or something. You have to overlook him, Corliss. He's got this thing about me – every time I sneeze, he just has a conniption fit!"

Corliss smiled. "I'm sure he's only looking out for your welfare."

"I suppose. Daddy's sweet." Jennie gave her a smile and picked up the tray. "Come along. Let's eat this while it still looks pretty. When it gets warm, it will go all flat."

The dessert was tasty. Reese delighted Jennie by asking for a second helping. Burr sat back and beamed. It was obvious how much he doted on his daughter. There was almost an unhealthy attachment. Whatever the girl wanted, Burr Kaldner would get for her, no matter what it took.

At last Reese and Corliss were able to

go. Burr shook their hands and let Jennie see them to the door.

"Oh, this was so much fun!" Jennie said. "Let's do it again."

"Thanks for the evening, Jennie. It was very nice," Reese said.

"Corliss, may I visit the lab sometime?"

Corliss was startled by the request. "Why, yes, of course. Just give me a call before you come."

"I will. Thank you. I'll see you soon. Real soon. Oh, Reese, wasn't it a really nice evening?"

Reese laughed at her enthusiasm. "Yes, it was."

"It was perfect. Goodnight!" She flung her arms around Reese's neck and kissed his cheek, and in a moment, Corliss was startled to find herself being embraced too. "Goodnight," Jennie said again. "Come again. Soon. Promise now. You hear?"

Corliss and Reese walked out into the night. As they drove away, they saw Jennie standing in the doorway in a wedge

73

of light, like a moth, poised for flight, waving to them.

"How can you be jealous of that?" Reese teased.

"Women are funny creatures. Sometimes they're not what they seem on the outside."

"Ah, no truer words were ever spoken," Reese said lightly.

They returned to the Town House, where Corliss had left her car.

"I'll follow you home," he said.

"No need. I'll be all right, and it's getting late."

"There's a prowler around. I don't like you going alone."

"I'll be all right!"

He scowled. "Still angry with me, aren't you?"

She gave him a stiff smile. "I'm glad the evening is over. Don't ever pull a surprise like that on me again."

They looked at each other for a moment, the air charged between them. This time, Reese relaxed first. He reached out to take her hand.

"Darling, why do we quarrel? Why do we waste time like this when we're together?"

Her temper faded. She found herself smiling. "Oh, I don't know, Reese."

"How soon can you leave your father? How soon can we go ahead with our plans?"

She heard the familiar longing in his voice, and as it always did, it touched and melted her heart and stirred her own longing. It put everything else into a hazy background and cut through to the heart and bone of the situation.

"Oh, Reese, if I only knew!"

With a quick motion, he pulled her to him. He kissed her ardently, and she clung to him.

"Make it soon, Corliss. Please!"

She drove slowly, in no real hurry to reach the house. As she reached Willow Woods, she took the twisting road with ease, knowing every turn and curve. Soon she was nearing Madeline Huffman's house. It was ablaze with lights. Perhaps she was having a party, although to

Corliss's knowledge, Madeline had never given a single party, luncheon, or tea since she'd moved here.

Was that a car in the drive? Drew's car!

For a moment, Corliss gripped the wheel tighter. What was Drew doing here at this time of night?

VI

Drew Fielding left his house in Willow Woods early every morning these days. With John Mitchell convalescing at home, he found more and more of the work coming to his desk. For the past year or more, ever since John's wife had died, John had been shifting the work to Drew's shoulders. Drew had found it a challenge. Filling John Mitchell's shoes wouldn't be easy for any man.

He enjoyed the early morning drives to Seabourne. The Mitchell plant was located on the east end of town in a brick building that had been expanded twice. But he didn't particularly enjoy the city, even if his work was there. Willow Woods was both a home and a haven. The house was his retreat. He did little entertaining. He bothered few of his neighbors with visits. When five o'clock came, he was content to go home, change clothes, and romp with Fuzz, or settle down with a good book in his den. Mrs. Petrie fed him ample and tasty meals. He was comfortably well off these days, thanks to John Mitchell; Mitchell Electronics was the largest employer in town, with Burr Kaldner coming along second. What more could a man want?

Drew bit down on the stem of his pipe whenever he thought about Burr Kaldner. He didn't like the man's tactics. Burr was quickly becoming a man of influence in Seabourne, but Drew still couldn't like him. Burr wasn't a man that he could trust, and after the way he had pulled a tricky maneuver to get the Dumont plant, Drew had even less respect for him.

Drew put his car in his reserved parking slot and said good morning to the guard as he went inside. He wasn't surprised to find Tom Whittier waiting for him.

"Hello, Drew."

"Problems?"

Tom nodded. He was a lean young

fellow, with bright eyes and hair beginning to thin on top. He was the best engineer at Mitchell Electronics. He had been put in charge of all their special projects. Drew had been dubious about it when John hired him. Tom's past record wasn't the best. The young man liked to gamble. Everyone knew his favorite hangout was Sadie's Place down on the riverfront, a supper club and bar with a back room where illegal gambling took place. It was one of those things that the city police chose to ignore.

Tom perched in a chair beside Drew's desk. "Not exactly a problem," he said. "I just wanted to check a few things with you. It's about the equipment for Doctor Gilman."

"What about it?"

The equipment was a sophisticated piece of machinery consisting of two units. Unit One had been designed and built by Paul himself . . .

"Well, it's going to cost more than I thought at first," Tom said.

Drew lighted his pipe and puffed at it

for a moment. He didn't like hearing this. Dr. Gilman was especially anxious to have this equipment built as quickly and inexpensively as possible. "Quite a lot more than the first estimate you made?" he asked.

"Afraid so. And I'll need more time."

Drew didn't like these kinds of problems. They were out of his field. He knew the law. He could manage the law. But suddenly to find himself running Mitchell Electronics was enough to frighten the best of men. John had managed things almost exclusively. He knew what was going on everywhere in the plant. In his own way, John Mitchell was a very remarkable man. He had always refused the idea of an assistant. "All I need is you, Drew," John used to say. "The rest are just accountants and clerks. You and me – we're the executive force here."

"I'll get in touch with Doctor Gilman, Tom," Drew said. "Write up a new estimate. Can you have it on my desk by noon?"

"Sure thing."

"Good. By the way, what do you think of the equipment?"

"What I've seen of it is great. But Gilman has kept Unit One under wraps. Sort of a big secret, I guess."

"New inventions have to be protected," Drew pointed out. "I know Paul's hoping to get a patent on this."

"I'll have to say Doctor Gilman is no dummy. He's got those designs figured out to a fare-thee-well!"

Drew smiled. "Paul studied engineering. In fact, there was a time he thought he would go into engineering. Then the research idea came along – and you know the rest. If he'd had time, I think Paul would have built Unit Two, too."

"I'll get right on the new estimate," Tom said.

Drew nodded and picked up a stack of paper work that had been carried over from yesterday. Tom disappeared. As Drew worked, he became aware of the sounds in the plant. People coming. Steps in the halls. The sounds of machines starting up. Another day was under way.

He pulled a curtain that covered a long window which overlooked the shop. From here he could check on things, and while he didn't believe in being a watchdog, he found it paid to take a look now and then. The mere presence of John Mitchell had always made things run smoother. He wasn't sure he could command the same sort of respect.

At ten o'clock, he phoned Dr. Gilman at the laboratory.

"There's been a snag, Paul. We're going to have to change the price of the equipment. Could I meet you for lunch?"

Paul sighed. "How much more?"

"I don't have the figures yet."

"All right. Lunch. Where?"

"The Seabourne Hotel. Twelve?"

"Fine."

Drew said goodbye and hung up. It wasn't like Tom to make an error even on preliminary plans. He hoped it wasn't going to be too high. Paul was a deserving man. He ran a top-notch laboratory, and he knew from Corliss that he was doing some important research work on the side.

The rest of the morning, Drew was busy with various conferences, made a few phone calls, and managed to slip away in time to meet Paul at the hotel.

Paul was late. While he waited, Drew drank coffee and thought about John Mitchell. It appeared it might be a long recovery. A shame. And hard on Corliss. He frowned, thinking about Corliss. She had never explained what she had been doing in Brightwell that day John had been taken ill. He wondered if Paul knew.

"Drew?" It was Paul Gilman.

Drew got to his feet.

"Sorry I'm late."

"It's all right."

They ordered, and then Paul got right to the point. "Do you have figures for me now?"

"Yes." Drew pulled out the estimate from his pocket and handed it across the table.

Paul looked at it and arched his brows. "So much?"

"Sorry. I wish we could hold it down,

but Tom's the engineer, and he knows what must be done to make it work."

"Another thousand dollars! I just don't know"

"If you'd like to get another bid—"

Paul made a wry face. "From Burr Kaldner? No, thank you. All right. Go ahead. How soon do you think you can have it ready?"

"A month. Six weeks. There are certain parts that must be ordered from abroad, according to Tom. Forgive my ignorance. I am, after all, just the company lawyer. If John were here—"

"How is Mitchell?" Dr. Gilman asked.

"Holding his own, but it's slow."

"Corliss is worried about him. I know that. But you have to admire that young woman. The more outside things bother her, the harder she works at the lab. She's like a woman possessed. I've even got her helping me with some of my experiments."

Drew took his pipe from his pocket and filled it with fragrant tobacco. "The other day, when her father took sick, she wasn't at the lab, was she?''

"No. She'd asked for some time off."

"Vacation?"

"I assume so," Paul said with a shrug. "I didn't really ask. It was none of my business."

Drew shook out his match and smiled. "Nor mine. Sorry."

They ate a companionable meal. Drew tried to talk about the equipment and its real purpose. Paul seemed reluctant to discuss it, and Drew began to get the feeling that it was something very important, perhaps very valuable. Was this why Paul had deliberately withheld information about the companion unit that went with the one Tom was building?

They parted at one o'clock. Paul hurried away to his lab, a harried, preoccupied man.

The rest of the day, Drew spent working at his desk, and when five o'clock came, he was nearly as relieved as the rest of the workers to close up shop and go home. But a bulging briefcase went with him. When he reached his house in Willow Woods, he found Fuzz waiting for him. With a laugh, he ruffled the dog's fur and walked toward the door.

"Supper's in ten minutes," Mrs. Petrie advised him.

"Good. I'm hungry."

"You're always hungry!" Mrs. Petrie said.

"It's just your good cooking, Mrs. Petrie."

"I know I'm a good cook, and I can keep a clean house. Am I going to lose my job?"

"What do you mean?"

Mrs. Petrie shrugged. "You may as well know. You're causing talk. You and that Widow Huffman."

He chose to ignore that remark. He changed into comfortable clothes and went back out to the table. This was the only part of his life he didn't like. Mrs. Petrie refused to eat with him, saying it wasn't her place. So he ate at the large table alone, looking out to the woods, watching the sun drop lower in the sky.

It was just dusk when he tucked the briefcase under his arm, whistled to Fuzz, and struck out through the woods toward the Mitchell place. Fuzz danced, circled, and barked as he ran ahead of him, chasing the squirrels and frightening the birds. Drew called him back. "Quiet down, you big ox. You're disrupting everything!"

The Mitchell house was larger than his, partly due to the small apartment to the rear where Sam and Martha Worth lived. He spied John out on the terrace, propped in a chair, and from there, he looked like a pale ghost. It gave Drew a start. He thought of John as a tall, vibrant man who walked and spoke quickly.

"Hello, John," Drew said.

John looked around. His eyes flashed with recognition.

"How are you?" Drew asked.

"How do you expect? I hate being an invalid, everyone creeping around, afraid they'll make a sound —" John broke off. He shook his head. "Sorry, Drew. I'm a miserable man to live with these days. What's in the briefcase?"

"Work. Things to discuss with you."

"I don't think I'm up to it."

Drew ignored that and opened the case anyway. He dropped a few things into John's lap. "Go over these at your leisure, will you? I'll get back to you on them later. Where's Corliss?"

"In the house."

"I'm stuck on this Walters matter, too," Drew said. "Shall we sign a contract with him or not?"

"Same terms?"

"Yes."

"Then, no, don't sign. If he won't agree to the new clauses in the contract – cancel him out."

Drew gave John a quick look. "We need his materials, John."

"He's not the only fish in the sea."

Drew gave the older man a smile. "I admire your nerve. I suppose that's why you're the boss, why you're the head of the company."

John clenched and unclenched his left fist. But he said nothing. Drew had been trying to appeal to the man's pride now for days, to stir him out of the melancholia he'd sunk into, but so far, it hadn't really worked.

"Hello, Drew."

Corliss stepped out to the terrace.

Sometimes, Drew suspected there were two women hiding inside Corliss. The one that spent long, dedicated hours at the lab but talked little about it except with her co-workers; this was Mitchell's daughter, aware of who she was, a woman rooted deep in the history and background of Willow Woods. Then there was the other Corliss, who laughed easily, who liked to tease, who walked rapidly as if she were eager to catch up with life itself, a happy, eager girl who reached out to everyone and everything. It struck Drew that one part of Corliss was very serious, old for her years, and the other was, if anything, very young, and perhaps even naïve.

"Am I interrupting something?" Corliss asked.

"Nearly finished," Drew said. "I'm going to leave a few things with your father. He can look over them tomorrow."

She gave him a grateful smile and said "Thank you" silently, barely moving her lips.

He snapped the briefcase shut. "How about a walk down the path, John? Fuzz will chase everything out of our way."

"No," John said tiredly. "Not tonight, Drew."

"You need a change of atmosphere. And the woods are their best this time of the day."

"Don't mollycoddle me!" John said, nearly shouting.

Drew nodded. "Sorry. Well, I think I'll be on my way then. See you tomorrow, John."

"I'll walk part way with you," Corliss said.

Fuzz was waiting for them. Corliss paused long enough to stroke his fur and rub his ears. Then they were off, dog and girl running, chasing each other, the girl laughing and the dog barking. Drew ambled behind them, smoking his pipe, enjoying the last light of the day. He caught up with them under a large old oak where long ago John Mitchell had built a small bench. Corliss was there, Fuzz sitting beside her, his head in her lap. "You spoil him," he scolded.

"Don't be silly. Every dog wants to be petted."

He sat down beside her. For a little while they sat companionably, not talking.

"Drew?"

"Yes?"

"How are things at the plant, really?"

"We're struggling along, but I miss your father, Corliss. He's the heart of things."

"He won't talk about what happened."

"It was a bitter pill to swallow, Corliss. Kaldner isn't one of his favorite people, you know."

"He blames Reese."

"Too bad."

"I wish there was something I could do."

"You're doing your share," Drew

pointed out. "Just by taking care of him, giving him something to look forward to every day. Your coming home at night must be a highlight for him."

"I don't know. I think he's angry with me too, because I'm in love with Reese—"

Drew gave her a quick look. "You never did tell me why you were in Brightwell that day."

She laughed, a quick, teasing laugh. "Why should I?"

"Curious, that's all."

"Well, Drew Fielding, you can go right on being curious!"

He leaned back against the trunk of the tree. The birds were settling in for the night. The sun had stained the sky a velvet red. A cool dew was beginning to fall in the woods. It pulled a lock of hair down to Corliss's forehead and curled another on the nape of her neck.

"Everyone goes to Brightwell to get married when they want to do it up fast," he said.

"Do they?"

He reached out and gripped her by the

shoulders. For a moment, he was angry enough with her to shake her as he had once when she was a teenager and needed it. She laughed. He let her go.

"You're a spoiled brat!" he said.

"So you've told me a dozen times."

He rapped his pipe out on the heel of his shoe and put it in his shirt pocket. Whistling to Fuzz, he got to his feet. "I'll drop by tomorrow for those papers I left for your father. Encourage him to look at them. It might help if he got his mind on something besides himself."

"I will. But you don't really need any kind of decision from him, do you?"

"No, but I thought —"

"Thank you, Drew, for making him feel needed."

He had moved but a couple of steps down the path when she called to him again.

"Drew! What are you doing so much at Madeline Huffman's house?"

Drew reached down to put his fingers into Fuzz's thick coat. "Curious?" he asked.

"Yes, I am."

He gave her a lift of his shoulders and a quick grin. "Then go right on being curious."

VII

Tom Whittler left the Mitchell plant with his pay envelope tucked in his shirt pocket. Whistling, he jumped into his red sports car, which still had several installments due, and roared out of the parking area. He'd checked out fifteen minutes early, and if Drew heard about it, or worse yet, the old man, he'd catch the devil for it. But he had plans for the evening, and he couldn't wait to get started. Big plans. He grinned to himself and reached up to pat the pay envelope. It had been a long time since he'd had any action, and tonight, come what might, he was going to find some.

He had supper at a favorite little restaurant. The food at Sadie's Place was only passable. But he liked the atmosphere there, and he liked the back room. More than likely, he'd play poker there

95

all night long. Unless he had a bad run of luck. Someday he was going to clean out that place. Take on every player that dared challenge him and turn their pockets out of every cent they had!

Sadie's Place was on the riverfront on the far edge of town, reached by a narrow graveled road, hidden in tall trees. It looked perfectly innocent. Only a very small sign over the door distinguished it. The house was a two-story frame building with a front porch and a screen door. Like someone's home. In fact, it was Sadie's home. Years ago, during some lean times, she'd decided to make the downstairs into a club, and she didn't particularly care who her patrons were as long as they crossed her palm with silver.

Tom was whistling as he turned in at the lane and drove back to the house. Still whistling, he bounced across the front porch and pulled open the door. Mosquitoes buzzed, and during hot summer nights, moths beat themselves against the screen, drawn by the light.

"Hi," Tom called.

Sadie was in evidence, complete with her orange wig, loose-fitting cotton dress, and comfortable sandals. At times she wore an apron, and always she wore gaudy beads. God knew, she was no answer to a man's dream, but she was a good sport and mothered them all. She was straight with everyone, she would tolerate no rowdiness, and she was good about carrying a man on credit – up to a point. After that, she could be as tough as nails.

"Long time no see," Sadie said with a wry grin. "Where you been?"

"Broke, that's where I've been," Tom replied. "How's my best girl?"

He put his arms around her and gave her a quick hug. She protested and bawled him out for it, but just the same, he knew she really liked the attention he gave her.

"Tell me, pet, any action tonight?" he asked.

"You're early. Just wait a little while."

"Okay," Tom grinned. "What's new around here?"

Sadie shrugged. "Nothing new. We're

like the river. We just keep rolling along."

Tom perched himself at a table again the wall and ordered coffee.

"Coffee?" Sadie said with mock surprise.

"Nothing stronger. Want to keep my wits about me tonight."

"Coffee," Sadie shrugged. "Hey, Max, bring the man coffee."

"Join me," Tom said.

"Listen, dearie, if I took time to sit down with all my customers, I wouldn't get anything else done."

Tom laughed. "Okay. Go about your merry way. I'll just sit here and be good and wait for things to start happening."

The coffee was hot and strong. Sadie didn't know how to make it any other way. But a bowl of pretzels helped, and as he whiled away the time, he took a small notebook out of his pocket. Inside it, he'd made a dozen different drawings, all of them concerning that tricky piece of equipment he was to build for Dr. Gilman. Fact was, he was excited about it. It had real potential. It dealt with blood analysis, and if it worked as Dr. Gilman expected, it would speed up things to a point where within a couple of minutes blood types could be matched, disease detected, blood count taken, and a dozen other tests completed.

He made a few notes and suddenly became aware of a shadow over his table. Glancing up, he was startled to find Burr Kaldner.

"Hello, boy, what's that?" Burr asked.

Tom hastily closed the notebook. "Just doodling," he said.

"Looked like diagrams to me. Plans. What is it? New product?"

"Not exactly."

Burr pulled a cigar out of his pocket and clipped the end off, then lighted it, watching Tom the whole time. "What's Mitchell pay you?"

"None of your business!" Tom got to his feet.

"I'd top it," Burr pressed. "Anytime. If you've some goodies there in that notebook."

Tom had heard about Burr's underhanded ways, but this was his first encounter with it personally. Before he could say anything, Burr moved away, shouting to Sadie. Sadie gripped Burr's arms and laughed up into his heavy face. "What you doing, Burr? Slumming? Used to be, you'd come here regular. What's the matter, too high-toned for us now?"

Burr put his arm around Sadie's shoulder and pulled her away. They talked for several minutes, heads together, occasionally bursting out into loud laughter. Tom pocketed the notebook and wished he'd left it home or in his desk at the office.

Business began to pick up. Mostly local men, only a few with women. And a few curious outsiders. Sadie's Place was one of the novelties of Seabourne. Notorious was a better name. Sadie ran a swinging place.

Tom noticed one of the men at the bar, sitting quietly, smoking, nursing one small drink. He was tall, thin as a rail, and had a big-city look about him. His clothes were a cut above average, but they needed tending. His suit needed pressing, and his shoes needed shining. He wore a thin moustache and dark glasses.

Tom went to sit on a stool beside him, taking his empty coffee cup with him. The man turned his head, but Tom couldn't see his eyes behind the dark glasses.

"Hi," the man nodded.

"You're new here."

"Sort of."

"Just move to Seabourne or passing through?"

"Passing through."

"Too bad," Tom grinned. "You really ought to get to know Sadie."

"I hear there's a few card games around here," the man said.

"There sure are. Want to sit in?"

"Why not? What else is there to do in this dump?"

Tom laughed shortly. "Seabourne isn't all that dead. Sleepy maybe, but not dead."

"I got a better word for it, but being a

polite guy by nature, I won't say it."

"Where are you from?" Tom asked.

"Never mind."

Tom lifted his brows. "Excuse me. Didn't mean to pry. Who told you about this place?"

"Oh, I heard," the man replied with a shrug. "When's the game start?"

"I'll check around," Tom said. "See you in the back room."

Tom moved around the room. He found a few more interested and went to speak to Sadie. She and Burr were still talking as if they were old, long-lost friends who had just rediscovered each other.

"Okay if we start a game?" he asked.

Sadie nodded. "Help yourself."

There, in a back room, on a round table, and under a lamp hanging directly over it, the players moved their chairs in with scraping sounds, and someone yelled to Sadie for a fresh deck of cards.

Tom found himself opposite the stranger who sat very quietly, looking at them all, slowly turning his head and appraising each man. There was something spooky about the guy.

The first game got under way. Tom broke even. A second started. Nothing very exciting happened. A third, fourth, a fifth game followed. Tom lost a little, recovered it, lost again. Sadie was in and out of the room with trays of drinks, sandwiches and coffee, and lingered long enough to see who was winning.

Others drifted in and out of the room. Once, Tom was aware of Burr Kaldner. He circled the table, staying in the shadows. He made Tom uneasy.

The stranger, who finally said his name was Cassiday, played a hard game. His face never changed in emotion. He never smiled, seldom spoke. His long-fingered hands held the cards with confidence. He began to win. Slowly, steadily.

At midnight, they broke for ten minutes, and Tom stepped out to the porch to get a breath of fresh air. From there, he could hear the river and smell it. The lights of Seabourne were to his left, stretched out like Christmas bulbs. He'd lost half of the money in his pay envelope.

At best, he could only play a couple more hands if he didn't start to win soon.

"What's the matter, honey?"

Sadie came out, linked her arm through his, and stared out to the night.

"Not doing so hot. Who is that guy? That Cassiday?" Tom asked.

"Wouldn't know for sure, but I think I've seen him before. A long time ago."

"Who is he? What's his business?"

Sadie shook her head. "Don't know. But the name Cassiday doesn't ring any bell with me. Still – I know that face. The clothes fooled me for a little while –"

"I didn't know you and Burr were so chummy."

Sadie laughed. "Dearie, I'm chummy with all of them. It's my business. Burr used to come here all the time before he got to be such an important man."

"What's he really like?"

"Granite," Sadie said. "Everything you hear about him is true. He's got one weak spot. His kid. Jennie. She's a grown young lady now, I reckon. I remember once, she got pneumonia and nearly died.

I thought Burr would go right out of his skull with worry."

"So the man's got a heart after all."

"He's got one, but only for Jennie. You'd do well to remember that. Anyone would."

"Too bad John Mitchell didn't realize that," Tom murmured.

"What did you say?"

"Nothing. Never mind. I'd better get back to the game."

"Good luck, sugar. You'll win the pot this time. I feel it in my bones."

He left the cool night air of the river and went inside to the smoke-filled room in the back. Cassiday was there, cool as a cucumber, waiting for the game to resume. Burr was still there too, leaning against the wall, arms folded. Tom sensed the two had been talking. Cassiday riffled the cards. The other players filed back into the room. Someone yelled at Sadie to bring more food.

One o'clock slipped by. Two o'clock. Tom was down to his last five dollars. The pot was a big one. He paused, looking at the cards in his hand. What did Cassiday have? Was he bluffing? Did he dare raise him the last five dollars?

He dared.

"Call," Cassiday said.

The muscles around Tom's chest tightened. He laid out his cards. Cassiday spread out his. Cassiday's lips twitched for the first time into a half smile.

"You lose," Cassiday said. He raked the pile of chips toward him. Tom lowered his head, feeling sick. His entire paycheck was gone.

"I'll give you a chance to get even," Cassiday said. "I'll take an I.O.U. if you want to stay in the game."

"How much?"

"I'll stake you to twenty-five dollars."

Tom licked his lips. He hated to leave, whipped. He had to win some of the money back. It was a long two weeks until another payday. "Okay. You're on."

The nightmare only grew worse. He lost that twenty-five and borrowed another. Soon, that too was gone. A circle of people had gathered to watch. The game was a hot one. A nerve type of thing. Tom won back ten. Twenty. His luck was changing!

Then abruptly, he found himself entangled again, the game down to Cassiday and himself. His luck ran out and suddenly he realized he was in hock to Cassiday for more than five hundred dollars. How had it happened? How could he ever pay up?

"That's it," Tom said. "I can't play anymore."

He stumbled out of the smoky room and straight through the bar to the fresh air outside. It was nearly dawn. The sky was pink. It was so quiet here now, he could hear the river. Steps sounded behind him. He whirled about. Cassiday stood there, a quiet shadow.

"You've got forty-eight hours to raise the money, mister," Cassiday said. "Leave it with Sadie. If you don't come up with it, I'll come looking for you."

"I'll get it!" Tom said.

"Be sure you do."

Then Cassiday walked away. For a

moment, Tom leaned against the porch railing, feeling sick. He heard rude laughter behind him. A cigar glowed in the darkness. He knew it was Burr Kaldner.

"Come work for me, Tom, and you'll get the money you need right off. A bonus."

Tom's stomach turned again. "No."

"I'll be around if you change your mind."

Tom muttered under his breath. He flicked away the beads of perspiration on his forehead. Burr left. His big, long limousine pulled away and disappeared down the graveled lane. Behind him, Sadie was closing the place for the night. The lights went out. Tom stumbled down the steps toward his car.

"Hey, Tom –"

He started. He thought everyone had gone.

"Who is it?"

"Alex Ward. I was watching the game."

"Oh, hi, Alex. Didn't know you were around."

"You were busy, man," Alex laughed. "Listen, I'll treat you to breakfast. Al's Diner. Okay?"

"Best offer I've had all night."

"See you there in ten minutes."

He'd met Alex Ward at a party several months ago. Alex was in and out of town every month. He traveled for a men's clothing firm.

Al's Diner was just a couple of notches above Sadie's Place. It stayed open all night and was located on the highway where truckers and late travelers often stopped. When Tom got there, Alex was waiting.

"What will you have?" Alex asked.

"Ham and eggs. Plenty of coffee."

Alex gave the order. He leaned back, a nice-looking guy with dark brown hair and blue eyes. He was a ladies' man. Everyone knew that. "You took a whipping back there," Alex said.

"I should know better. Who is that Cassiday anyway?"

Alex shrugged. "Never seen him before. But he's got his hooks in you."

109

"And how!" Tom lamented.

"What if Mitchell hears about this?"

"Mitchell's sick. He's not in the office. Drew Fielding is running the show. But he's not much better."

"That's one thing about my job." Alex laughed. "I don't have a boss breathing down my neck every minute of the day. While I'm on the road, I'm on my own."

"And what a way to go! Tell me, you still dating Elizabeth Lane?"

Alex frowned. "No."

"But I thought—"

"Elizabeth's a nice gal. For a while, I thought maybe I could go for her in a big way. But—well, you know."

"Sure."

Personally, Tom thought Elizabeth was one of the nicest girls he knew. Corliss Mitchell was okay, too, but she was already spoken for, and besides, she was the boss's daughter.

"The last time I saw Elizabeth, she said Gilman was neck deep in research. She and Corliss Mitchell were really running the lab. That true?" Alex asked.

"Probably. Gilman's working on a new piece of test equipment. In fact, I'm designing part of it."

Alex leaned toward him. "Something important?"

"I think so."

"Hey, that might make a big man out of you!"

"Doubt it. Right now, I feel two inches tall."

"What you need is a winning streak."

"I need to go home and soak my head!"

"Cheer up, fella. Tomorrow will look better."

Tom ate the breakfast Alex bought him. They gossiped about the women in town, Mitchell's illness, Burr Kaldner's growing influence, and things in general. When they parted, it was nearly seven o'clock. Tom went home. There was time to shower and shave before reporting to work. He began emptying his pockets. Fingering the notebook, he flipped it open for a moment and studied the drawings he'd made last night. It might work. It

111

had to work! But he wished he knew about the other unit, the one Gilman had made himself. He'd like a look at it, out of curiosity's sake, if nothing else. But Gilman had been close-mouthed about it, refusing to tell him anything.

He sensed that the whole design was very important, very valuable. Did Kaldner know something about it? Hadn't he been overly interested last night? It worried him. Kaldner had ways of getting what he wanted. He wondered if he should tell Drew about it. Then in the next moment, he knew he couldn't. Drew didn't like his after-work behavior. He'd made it plain. Not once. Several times.

"No," Tom muttered. "I'll have to ride this one out alone."

VIII

Corliss took each day as it came. It was as if she had suddenly divided her heart into three parts. Reese, her father, and the lab. She spent as much time with her father as she could, and he seemed to be slowly improving. He walked about the house with a cane, and occasionally took a short stroll along one of the many paths.

As for Reese, she was meeting him away from the house, usually in Seabourne. By necessity her meetings with him were fewer than in the past, a fact he both understood and resented.

When they saw each other alone, Corliss found herself going straight into his arms. It seemed their love grew more desperate each day.

"We can't go on like this, Corliss," Reese said. "Slipping around, meeting as if this were some clandestine affair!"

"What can I do?"

"I'm coming to the house. Your father has to face me sometime."

She put her fingers on his firm lips, tears stinging her eyes. "Not yet, darling. Father's just not ready. I don't want him to have a setback."

Reese's eyes flashed at that, and he pulled her closer. "Let's go back to Brightwell. I still have the license. It's still valid. There would be nothing he could do about it."

"I can't. Oh, I can't, Reese! You know I can't. Don't make it any harder than it already is." She looked into Reese's dark green eyes and saw the hunger on his face. It twisted her heart, and she touched the lines in his brow, smoothing them away. "I'm doing all I can, Reese. You must know that."

Reese relaxed. A storm of emotion went across his face. He took a deep breath. "I'm sorry. I don't mean to do this to you. It's just that I love you. I want to marry you. Now! I don't want to wait any longer. Darling, what are we going to do?"

She had no answers. Nor did he. They could only cling wordlessly to each other and try to hope, to find the strength they needed in each other.

"It's ironic," he said at last. "At first, you wanted to be married, and I was stubborn. I had to have everything just right in my world. Now, I'm ready, and you're not."

She reminded him of something he had told her long ago. "Remember, Reese, you said there would be a time for us. I still believe that. So must you."

"Your father will have to face me one of these days! We can't go on forever like this."

"He will, when the time's right. I promise."

But when was that going to be? She didn't want to tell Reese that anytime she tried to approach the subject, her father reacted strongly. Often he simply got up and went to his room, closing the door tightly behind him. Once he had gone into a rage, and for the next three days he had been morose and depressed. She had feared she would have to phone the doctor.

What was she going to do about it? What could she do? It was like walking a tightrope between the two. Loving Reese, needing him, but feeling protective of her father, knowing that he too needed her. How could she turn away from him? To see a man like John Mitchell, a giant in his own right, suddenly felled, reduced to long, empty days, walking on a cane, was not easy.

Oh, how long? she wondered sometimes during sleepless, restless nights. How much longer?

Her only real solace was the lab. She could lose herself there, brush aside all the difficulties of her life. At the lab, black was black and white was white. A fact was a fact. It either was or wasn't. Without the lab to steady her, she wasn't sure she could have continued to walk the tight-rope.

She usually left the house early every morning, enjoying the drive through Willow Woods to Seabourne and the lab.

But one particularly lovely day, she was late and took the curves a little faster than usual. Suddenly she saw someone in the path of her car.

"Oh, look out!" she screamed.

She hit the brakes. Dust flew. The man leaped aside. Her car swerved. Somehow, she twisted and fought the wheel and brought the car under control.

It had frightened her so much that for a moment she could only sit there, clutching the wheel, breathing hard. She had nearly struck a man! Then she put the car in reverse and went back. But there was no one there!

"That's strange," she murmured. "Where on earth did he go?"

Had she given him such a fright that he had simply ducked away in the woods? Odd. He had been a tall man, and while she had caught only a fleeting glimpse, she was certain he had been a stranger to the woods.

The prowler! The thought leaped into her head with terrifying aspects. She put the car in gear and drove away quickly, suddenly feeling frightened and uneasy. There hadn't been any recent reports of new thefts, but she knew that everyone was still edgy. She sped out of Willow Woods, relieved when she reached the open highway.

At best, her nerves were not steady these days, and it was hard to brush the incident out of her mind. It was still very much with her as she reached the lab and went inside.

Elizabeth was there, busy at her desk.

"Hello, Elizabeth. I'm late, aren't I?"

"Just a few minutes. Is something wrong? You look –"

"I'm all right," Corliss said quickly. "Really I am."

Elizabeth's brown eyes were kind and sympathetic. "No, you're not. I know what a spot you're in, and it can't be much fun."

Corliss tried to smile. "Drew said it will all come out in the wash."

"Let's hope he knows."

"Is Paul here?"

Elizabeth laughed. "Hours ago."

She went down the hall and found him at his desk, poring over a set of complicated designs. She bent over his shoulder for a quick look at the drawings. They meant little to her. "You amaze me, Paul. With a mind like this, why did you decide to be a lab man?"

Paul smiled. "I had two ambitions. To be an electrical engineer or a doctor. I ended up being neither, but brushing elbows with both."

"Can you get a patent on all of this?"

Paul rerolled the plans, put them in a cardboard tube, and locked them in a wall safe. "I'm hoping. It could make some real money for me and the lab. You remember the government grant I applied for? I haven't heard a word. It doesn't look very promising."

"It's just not fair!" she protested. "You deserve some financial help, Paul."

"I have these reports ready for your final analysis. When you've completed them, bring them back, and we'll review them."

When Corliss went back to the lab, Elizabeth was just hanging up the phone. She looked pensive, uncertain.

"That was Alex," she said. "He wants the four of us to go out to dinner tonight. Could you and Reese go?"

"Probably. But are you sure you want to see Alex?"

"He's fun. He can be very nice."

"He can also make a wreck out of you," Corliss pointed out. "Listen, honey, I just don't want him to hurt you again."

"That was my fault," Elizabeth said. "I read too much into our dates."

Corliss reminded herself it was Elizabeth's affair, not hers.

"I'll phone Reese," Corliss said.

When her call was put through to Reese's office, a strange, feminine voice answered. It wasn't his secretary, she was certain of that.

"May I speak to Mr. Sheridan, please?"

"May I ask who's calling?"

"Corliss Mitchell."

120

"Corliss. Hi! This is Jennie Kaldner. I'm here bothering Reese. Daddy gets mad at me for barging in uninvited, but I get bored at home. I'll let you talk to Reese."

In a moment, she heard Reese's voice on the line.

"I'm sorry if I interrupted when you were busy," she said.

"Don't be silly," he said, and there was instant anger in his voice.

She explained quickly about Alex Ward's invitation.

"Of course we'll go! It's high time you had some fun."

"I'll meet you here at the lab. About seven."

"Corliss, it's time I came to the house and picked you up!"

"I don't want to argue about it now. We've gone all through this a dozen times. I thought we'd agreed. I'll be here at the lab."

She hung up before he could argue any further. She wondered what Jennie Kaldner was doing in Reese's office so

121

early in the day. Was this a habit of hers, dropping in like that?

The day's work was routine. Corliss concentrated fiercely, shutting out the rest of the world. She spent the afternoon with Paul's research material. She had such an overwhelming hunch about Paul Gilman's promise, and it thrilled her to think she was a part of his lab.

When she got home, she went straight out to the terrace. Father was in a lawn chair, busily examining the files Drew had left him a few minutes earlier. She bent over to kiss his cheek.

"Have a good day?"

"Fair." He frowned. "I'm a little tired."

"I won't be able to join you for dinner tonight. I'm going out with Elizabeth and her friend. But I'll have coffee before I go."

Before he could argue or show disappointment, she went to her room. She was tired. Bone tired. It was a constant war of nerves, pacifying her father when she went out with Reese and pacifying

Reese because she had so little time for him.

A few minutes after six, she joined Father on the terrace where Martha had served him dinner. She helped herself to a cup of coffee. Father was picking at his food, and he refused to look at her. Her heart gave a tired wrench. He didn't want her to go. Of course he suspected that Reese too was part of the evening.

"Father—"

"Did I hear the doorbell?" Father asked, raising his head.

She heard the murmur of voices and then the sound of footsteps coming across the terrace. Her heart all but stopped. It was Reese! He came striding toward them, shoulders set with determination, a hard shine in his eyes.

"Good evening, sir," Reese said.

Corliss couldn't find her tongue. She couldn't move. Reese had dared to take matters into his own hands. She was sick with the thought of the consequences. She looked at her father. He sat like a man made of wood, watching Reese.

"How are you, sir?" Reese asked. "Corliss tells me you are making great improvements."

For a terrified moment, Corliss feared her father would simply get up and walk away. But she had forgotten that there was a basic courage to her father, that there was steel in his makeup. He was not a man to run when the going got tough.

"Thank you for your concern," Father said at last. His voice was laced with sarcasm and color came into Reese's face as if he'd just been slapped on both cheeks.

"Whether you choose to believe it or not, it's sincere," Reese said in a steady voice. "I'm sorry it has worked out this way and that there are hard feelings."

"I'm sure Burr couldn't care less!" Father said.

"I'm not Burr," Reese pointed out quietly.

The two men locked glances.

"I remember something you told me once, John," Reese said. "You told me that when you're in business, business has to come first, no matter what, if you want to be successful."

"There are ways of making business come first which are good and decent and respected. Then there are other ways—"

Reese straightened. "I haven't come to quarrel. Only to tell you I'm sorry you've been ill and to hope that you'll make a speedy and thorough recovery. Now, we have friends waiting. Goodnight!"

Reese took Corliss by the arm and walked away with her. Their steps echoed hollowly on the flagstone terrace. Without a word, Reese propelled her through the cool house and outside to his car.

"Reese, were you out of your mind? I thought we agreed—"

"It was time." Reese's hand gripped her arm all the more tightly. "He has to know that he isn't scaring me away. He has to know that I'm not giving you up for anyone or anything! I think he understands that now."

"Reese, do you really think so?"

Reese nodded. He pulled her close. He kissed her recklessly, eagerly. "I won't have it any other way," he said. "Now, we're going out. We're going to have a good time. Nothing's ever going to come between us again. That's the way it's going to be. Put your mind to it – and your heart!"

IX

The night fell softly around them. Dusk was a favorite time of day for Corliss. Everything in Willow Woods took on a certain hush as birds settled in for the night, calling to their young, and small animals scurried into the trees and hid themselves. But tonight it seemed especially beautiful, especially enchanting. For hope was beating sweet and sure in her heart. Reese had taken matters into his own hands, and she believed that only good could come from it.

"Oh, Reese, I feel as if I were standing right on the edge of a very high mountain with the whole world at my feet!"

Reese pulled her close and brushed his lips across her forehead. "I know, darling. I feel the same way."

They sped along through Willow Woods, and when they passed the spot where only that morning Corliss had seen the strange man, she told Reese about it.

"It's summer. There are a great many people traveling all over the country. Perhaps someone was just out hiking," Reese said.

"I keep thinking about the prowler."

Reese frowned. "Is there still talk about that?"

"Yes."

"I want you to be careful driving home alone. Keep the car doors locked."

"I wonder what anyone could want in Willow Woods?"

"There are nice homes here," Reese said. "People have nice things in their houses. It could tempt a petty thief all right."

"Oh, let's not think about it tonight, Reese."

He laughed. She was aware that both of them were floating on the air. Perhaps they were presuming too much. But she wouldn't think about that either.

"I'd rather we were going alone tonight," Corliss said.

"I thought it was all off between Alex and Elizabeth."

"I thought so too. But the very minute Alex calls, Elizabeth goes limp. She's been hurt badly by Alex, I don't want to see her hurt again."

"She's a grown woman," Reese laughed. "She knows what she's doing."

"Alex has her bewitched."

Reese gave her a teasing smile. "And do I have you bewitched? Do you go limp when I phone?"

Corliss frowned. "Except when I find Jennie Kaldner in your office."

Reese gave her a quick look. "Now, Corliss—"

"What was she doing there this morning? Does she drop by often?"

"Oh, all the time. She goes to lunch with me, helps me with my mail, takes phone messages—"

"I could scratch her eyes out," Corliss said. "Even if she is a sweet girl!"

"That's just exactly what she is. A sweet kid. Now, let's drop the subject, shall we?" Reese said. "We're not going to let anything spoil tonight."

Corliss forgot Jennie Kaldner, her father, all the problems that had been crowding her world, and concentrated on Reese and the evening ahead. Alex and Elizabeth were going to meet them at the Royal Club. Half an hour later, they had arrived. They parked their car and went inside. Alex and Elizabeth were waiting for them.

They talked about usual things, the best food on the menu, the common acquaintances they knew, the hot, dry weather – and Reese and Alex discussed business.

"My business is slow," Alex confessed. "It always is this time of year. But of course, these two girls are keeping their noses close to their microscopes."

"We have been exceptionally busy," Elizabeth said. "Paul does almost none of the daily reports these days. He's deep in his research."

"How does the man endure it?" Alex asked. "Hours and hours and hours of accomplishing nothing."

"That's not true?" Corliss protested.

Alex lifted his dark brows. "But what has he found? A new germ? A new pill? A new disease? A cure?"

"No, but—"

"Well then?" Alex asked with a smile. "You're being much too melodramatic about this, Corliss."

"Perhaps you're being shortsighted," Corliss said.

Alex lighted a cigarette and snapped off his gold lighter.

"Now, if the man could discover a new antibiotic or a cure for cancer – why even a cure for the common cold – then I'd sit up and take notice. But as it is, he's just growing musty there in his little lab, working two beautiful young ladies half to death!"

"Oh, Alex," Elizabeth laughed. "You always exaggerate everything. Stop teasing."

But Corliss didn't think Alex was teasing. He was serious. Only Elizabeth, her eyes dusted with stars, didn't realize this. She didn't hear the touch of sarcasm in

Alex's words, the contempt. Alex was the kind that would find something unpleasant to say about almost anything he didn't truly understand.

"By the way, did Gilman ever marry? Or is he still a bachelor?" Alex asked.

"He's a bachelor," Elizabeth said. "Why?"

Alex shrugged. "No reason. He was always sort of a spooky guy to me. I can't dig these dedicated people."

"He's going to be an important man someday," Elizabeth said warmly. "If not with a discovery in his research lab, then with the new equipment he's designed."

Alex looked interested. "A lab man builds equipment? What kind of equipment?"

"There are two units. One he has already built himself. The other has been turned over to Tom Whittier at Mitchell Electronics—"

Reese raised his brows at Corliss. "You never told me about that?"

"I think we've talked enough shop,"

Corliss said.

"What is it, a big dark secret?" Alex asked.

"No. But if we don't order some food soon, I'm going to starve to death!"

Everyone laughed, and at last they talked of something else. Corliss knew how Paul felt about his equipment. He was secretive about it and probably with just cause. It just seemed best not to discuss it, even among friends.

When the dance music started, Reese reached across the table to Corliss, the light deep and bright in his eyes. "Come on, darling."

She moved into his arms. Reese smiled down at her and brushed his lips across her forehead. "Let's leave as soon as we can," he said. "I think I want to be alone with you."

"Yes," she said.

Her heart was singing. For the first time since her father had been taken ill, she felt happy. They spun around the floor, laughing, and Corliss wanted the night never to end.

"Having fun?" Reese asked.

"Need you ask?"

"No."

He held her closer. They forgot everything but each other. It came as a kind of shock when Alex appeared beside them and tapped Reese's shoulder.

"Change partners, old boy."

She didn't want to let Reese go. She didn't want to dance with Alex. But Reese gave her a nod and an apologetic smile.

Alex wasn't as tall as Reese. Corliss found that his eyes were on the same level as hers. They were a quick, bright blue, and they unnerved her.

"You don't like me, do you, Corliss?" Alex asked.

She was so startled that she missed a step. "Don't be silly."

"I'm not. Why? Most women do."

"All right. If you insist. I don't like what you're doing to Elizabeth. She's a dear friend, and I don't like to see her hurt."

"Elizabeth is a sweet girl." Alex's smile was cool. "I like her very much. If

134

she chooses to put more emphasis on our relationship than that—"

Corliss stopped dancing, furious at his blatant casualness. "I'd like to go back to the table."

Alex measured her with his bright eyes and took her arm. "If you prefer."

The music stopped. Somehow, the four got through the meal. Now and then, Reese gave Corliss a puzzled look. Alex was, as usual, talking too much, monopolizing the conversation, and charming Elizabeth all the more. He was such a phony! Why couldn't Elizabeth see it?

"Well, look who's here!" Alex said, looking up. A large group was being seated across the room. Most of them were well-known citizens of Seabourne. Alex excused himself and went directly to the group. He busily shook hands and slapped backs and smiled engagingly at all the women. Elizabeth watched silently, a tiny frown on her face.

"Isn't that Madeline Huffman?" Reese asked. "The woman who lives in Willow Woods?"

Corliss turned about for a quick look. "Yes, that's Madeline."

In a moment, Alex was back. "They want us to join them. Come along. Just for a little while."

Elizabeth hung back. She was disappointed with this turn of events. She knew from past experience what would happen. Before the night was over, Alex was apt to forget all about her. He was that way in a crowd.

Corliss didn't want to go either. Nor did Reese. But Alex made it difficult to say no. There were introductions and friendly greetings.

Madeline was much lovelier than Corliss remembered from their first and brief meeting some months ago. Her hair was very blonde, very soft, very well done. Her blue eyes were clear, specked with bits of silver, and her lips were full, parting often in a pretty smile.

"I didn't realize you and Drew were such good friends," Corliss said pointedly.

"Oh, he's a joy, isn't he? A real joy.

Your father must feel very fortunate to have him to take over the plant when he needed him so much."

"He's like a son to Father."

Madeline Huffman smiled again, but it was a cool, distant smile. It was a smile that Corliss didn't trust. There was no real warmth in it.

"I wasn't sure I'd like Willow Woods," Madeline was saying. "It seemed so remote and quaint. Yet, I wanted to get away from the city. I wanted the peace and quiet, if you know what I mean. And Roberts Mill! Oh, what a lovely place that is."

A bracelet sparkled on Madeline's wrist. A ring with a large gem graced her finger. They were very smooth, white hands. They had probably never done any kind of work at all. Never planted a flower or pruned a tree or stirred a cake for the oven. They wouldn't know what to do with a typewriter or needle and thread or a test tube.

"I've talked to several in Willow Woods about my idea, Corliss. I haven't wanted to bother you and your father. Have you heard about it?"

"No. I haven't."

"The old mill! It must be restored. It's crumbling and falling down. Such a beautiful old thing. I've started a little program to save it."

"I don't understand."

"First, we have to raise funds. I'm working on that right now."

Corliss thought of the mill. The cool shadows there. The green pool where she and Reese as children had met and fell in love. It annoyed her to think of strangers there, tramping all over the place, changing it, ruining it.

"I love the mill, just as it is," Corliss said defensively.

"But we must be practical, Corliss. It's simply going to rot away! First, we'll form a local organization and buy it."

Corliss was annoyed. "I'm sure Drew could best advise you about that!"

Madeline laughed and reached up to tuck away a blonde wisp of hair. "Yes. I'm sure he can. I'll be in touch with him about it. I can assure you of that.''

Corliss looked for Reese. She wanted to go. Now. Her head was beginning to ache. She didn't want to talk to Madeline any more or hear how her voice grew soft when she mentioned Drew's name. The evening had started out so nicely, but where had the magic gone?

X

Leaving the Royal Club, Reese found Corliss quiet, almost remote. He stretched out his hand to touch her.

"What is it?"

"Nothing. Sorry. Really, nothing."

"You're so far away."

She moved closer. In a moment, her head was on his shoulder. Her soft hair brushed his face, and he was aware of her perfume, light and sweet, like the woman herself. But there was something about Madeline Huffman that was bothering her. He knew her too well. He had seen them talking together and overheard Madeline's plans to restore the old mill.

"You resent Madeline's interest in Roberts Mill, don't you?" Reese asked.

"Yes. She'll probably ruin it!"

Reese laughed. "You're exaggerating."

"I think Madeline Huffman just wants to get her name in the paper. Make a big splash."

"She does seem the type."

"She'll head all the committees, grab all the glory, and do none of the work. I just wish she'd leave things alone!"

Corliss usually had an objective view about most things. She was no one's fool. There was in her the same streak of good horse sense that men found in her father. How else had John Mitchell built up such a profitable enterprise? He admired the man, but he could not say this to Burr Kaldner. Burr wanted to nudge John off the pedestal in Seabourne. He might even succeed in doing it. But Burr would never have the style and class of John Mitchell, no matter how many expensive cars he drove and how many big cigars he smoked. Burr was a rough-cut gem, and he could be polished only to a certain extent.

Reese tightened his arm around Corliss. Sometimes it was hard to believe, even now, that she belonged to him.

"I remember how you were that first day I saw you at the mill, Corliss," Reese said. "You were like a wild-flower, long-stemmed, fragrant, sheltered from the sun, and yet of the open sky. You were there, just for me to reach out and pluck."

"You make me sound easy. I didn't exactly swoon at your feet."

He laughed. "No. At first I was a little afraid of you."

"And you fascinated me," Corliss said. "You looked so angry and hungry and determined. There was a chip on your shoulder. I ached to knock it off."

"It's off," he said quietly. "It's been off for a long time."

"Sometimes I wonder."

"You're thinking about earlier this evening? With your father?"

"Yes."

"It was the only way to handle him, Corliss. John Mitchell is a man who admires another man only when he stands up on his own two feet. I had to be firm with him. If I had let him steamroller me tonight, it would never have been right

142

again."

"I suppose not. But I worry about him. He's on an edge, Reese. Even if he pretends he isn't."

"Maybe it's time for him to step down."

Corliss pulled away from him and smoothed her hair. "So a man like Burr can step in?"

"No," Reese said. "I didn't mean that. There's always Drew. Your father has trained him well."

"But Drew is a lawyer. He loves the law. He's not comfortable in Father's chair."

Reese didn't like Drew Fielding. He never had, and he never would. Drew had everything. A nice house. Friends. A good position. Money. Respect. He'd come to Seabourne ten years ago, and look where he was now. Reese wondered if he could do as well in the same length of time. Most of all, he resented the way Drew fit into the Mitchell business, the Mitchell family. He knew Drew had come from a good family upstate, but that he'd actually had little when he came here. Still, there was that look about him that said he'd done all the right things, gone to the right schools, knew the right people, and had known instinctively from birth which fork to use.

They rode silently through the night, winding their way through the curving roads of the woods. At last, they reached Corliss's house. He shut off the motor and drew Corliss close in an urgent, reckless manner. She was all softness in his arms, frailer than she looked, with sweet lips and a fervor that matched his own. She broke away.

"How much longer must we wait? When can we go ahead with our plans?" he asked impatiently.

"As soon as possible. Now, walk me to the door. Please."

They walked to the house, arms around each other. The house was a solid shadow waiting for them. Inside, a night light burned. The smell of Sam Worth's rose beds was heavy in the air, sweet, tantalizing.

One last kiss, one last sweet moment of

holding her close and then she was gone, lost into the dark house. For a moment, he waited. Then he saw the light come on in her room, and he had a crazy urge to go after her, to carry her away, to drive to Brightwell and find that funny old J.P. again.

A cool breeze smoothed its way over his face. He knotted his fists, swore quietly, and went back to the car. Wait. He would have to wait! All his life, it seemed, he had been waiting for something.

"For everything," he muttered to himself. "For everything!"

It was not terribly late. He was restless. The thought of returning to his apartment was not appetizing. He could drop by Burr's house, but he quickly dismissed that idea. As he drove back to Seabourne, he found himself taking a road that had once been familiar. Years ago he had lived in this area. He turned down Fulton Street. The house where he had lived was gone now, making way for a new housing development. But the neighborhood hadn't really changed. He felt the ache of those days go through him.

Sadie's Place was not new to him. But it had been a long time since he had been there. Once he had served as Sadie's errand boy. In return she had given him a few hot meals and some decent clothes. He'd always have a warm spot in his heart for her. He drove there and got out.

Sadie's Place wasn't busy. Things didn't usually get rolling here until the wee hours. He caught a glimpse of the river glinting in the starlight. To the north were heavy thunder clouds. Perhaps before morning, they'd have rain. He walked across the front porch at Sadie's, and the door thumped behind him. He paused to look around.

"Well, well, well!"

He grinned, watching Sadie come strutting across the room to him, her cotton skirt swishing, her orange hair garish in the dim light. A jukebox was blaring. The room was smoky despite the air conditioning.

"Hello, Sadie. How are you?"

"I'm survivin'," she retorted,

punching a fat forefinger against his shoulder. "And you – real sporty these days, I hear."

"Am I? Or am I just a river rat after all?"

Sadie made a face and linked her arm through his. "Come on. We'll talk. Hey, Max!" she shouted. "Bring us something cool to drink."

Sadie ousted someone from a small table. "Use the bar, buster. Me and my friend want to sit here."

The man shrugged and ambled away. They were used to Sadie's direct ways and none dared to cross her.

Sadie did most of the talking. Reese leaned back, smoking quietly, listening. Most of Sadie's talk was about people they both knew, her business, her ideas of enlarging the place.

"Don't," he shook his head. "You'd spoil the whole effect. Don't you know how it is, Sadie? Most men who come here look upon it as a second home. This old house, the front porch, even the squeaky screen door – it takes us all back."

Sadie puckered her lips and nodded. "Yeah, maybe you're right. Maybe I won't change a thing."

"Is there a game going on in the back room?"

"Sure. You want in?"

"No."

"You never did go for the cards, did you?"

"No."

"Too smart!" Sadie grinned. "You always figured the angles, Reese Sheridan."

He frowned at that. "I've got certain things to do, Sadie, and I aim to do them, one way or another."

Someone shouted to Sadie, and she left. Reese leaned back, waiting, looking around him. He knew Burr still came here occasionally, but not often. Still, it was a place to Burr's liking. Smoky, noisy, filled with man talk, occasionally a little excitement in the form of a fight – which Sadie always broke up in her own inimitable way. She kept a loaded shotgun under the bar. At least she claimed it was loaded.

No man felt easy facing a load of buckshot. It usually cooled tempers very quickly. Sadie, if not subtle, was forceful.

Sadie returned. She had a checkerboard under her arm. Reese laughed.

"You remembered!" he said with surprise.

"You were the darnedest young sprout I ever knew for checkers. I could beat you then, I can beat you now," Sadie laughed.

They set up the board. Reese leaned forward, marking out his plays in his mind.

"Sadie!"

Someone had stopped at the table. A tall man. A stranger to him. Yet, somehow, he seemed familiar. He wore dark, expensive clothes, and his eyes were hidden behind huge sunglasses. What did he wear them for now, in the dead of night?

"Oh, hello, Cassiday," Sadie said.

"You got anything for me? Did that fella pay up?"

"Tom Whittier is broke. Stone, flat broke," Sadie said. "Give him a little

149

time."

Reese looked up, suddenly very interested in the conversation.

"He's had time. All the time he was allowed," Cassiday replied coldly. "Where do I find him?"

Sadie ignored the man, moving a checker into a new place on the board.

Cassiday got angry. "I asked you a question, Sadie!"

Sadie eyed him. "Listen, mister, I don't play detective. And I don't mix into people's quarrels. So, Tom lost some money to you. It's your headache, not mine."

"Where do I find him?"

"I don't know where he lives." Sadie shrugged. "Ask around. Look in the phone book. Just amble out of here, Cassiday, or I'll go get my shotgun."

Cassiday stared at her incredulously. "You've got to be kidding, lady."

"She's not kidding, mister," Reese said. "She'd as soon fill you full of buckshot as look at you if you aim to make any kind of trouble. One thing about Sadie.

She runs a straight place here."

A crowd began to gather around them. Cassiday looked about him nervously. His lips worked, and he pulled his black moustache. Then, with a duck of his head, he pushed through the crowd and made for the door. The screen swished shut behind him.

"How much does Tom Whittier owe Cassiday?" Reese asked.

"Don't know for sure," Sadie replied. "Several hundred. He was to have had it here last night."

Reese thought for a moment. Then he gripped Sadie's shoulder and smiled at her.

"See you another time, Sadie. We'll finish that game."

Then, as Cassiday had done, Reese pushed through the crowd and stepped out to the front porch. A moth struck him in the face, and he flicked it away. He hurried out into the darkness, hearing Cassiday's footsteps just ahead of him.

XI

Corliss heard Reese's car drive away. She went out to Martha's immaculately kept kitchen. She was surprised to find her father there, pouring a glass of milk.

"Hi! You had the same idea, I see."

"You're home early," he said.

"Yes."

"Reese is a hot-headed young man," Father said peevishly. "Bursting in here tonight, proud as a peacock!"

She felt all hope begin to explode and disintegrate. She had been so sure – so optimistic –

"I suppose I haven't really been fair," Father sighed. "Reese has a point. Business is business. It's just unfortunate that he's working for a man like Burr. I'm sorely afraid some of Burr's tactics will rub off on him."

She was surprised. "Then you're not

angry?"

"Not pleased, naturally, but no, I'm no longer angry. I'll try to treat that young man politely if nothing else."

"Oh, Father!" She went to him with a rush and put her arms around his neck in a cheerful hug.

"I only ask that you don't rush into anything, Corliss. I'd like both feet under me before you do anything rash. Now, let's go to bed. Tomorrow's another day."

The next morning, Corliss drove to Seabourne, humming. She didn't mind the bothersome heavy traffic, the noisy city. The lab waited for her. She was in love with it, with everyone, with the world!

But one look at Elizabeth's face and some of her happiness died. "I can guess! Alex Ward!"

"He was terribly busy with Madeline Huffman after you and Reese left last night," Elizabeth said unhappily.

"I thought you weren't going to let this bother you, Elizabeth."

"I'm trying," she said.

"That skunk!"

Elizabeth smiled wanly. "Well, I asked for it. Alex's not going to change. Ever. Why can't I make myself believe it?"

"You will. In time. And I have news! Father was positively sweet last night about Reese. They patched things up."

The phone rang, Corliss went to answer it.

"Hello, darling."

"Reese!"

He laughed. "I like the way you say my name."

"I love saying it. Reese, I can't wait to see you –"

"I've only got a minute, hardly that. I'm sorry. I can't make our luncheon date, and I'm going to be tied up tonight too."

"Oh, Reese. No!"

"Sorry."

"But I want to tell you about Father!"

"What about him?" he asked impatiently. "Really, I've got to run –"

"It's all right. Reese, do you understand, it's all right! He's willing to patch it up."

There was a surprised silence on the other end. "Well, I'll be damned," Reese muttered.

"Isn't it great?"

"Wonderful, darling. It really is. But I've got to run. I'm late now."

"Did I hear Jennie in the background? Is she there with you?"

"I'll call tomorrow. Goodbye."

Then the line went dead. Corliss hung up with a frown. If Reese was tied up with a business meeting, what was Jennie doing there? She had heard Jennie's voice, hadn't she?

After a moment of thought, Corliss reached for the phone and dialed her father's office and asked for Drew. In a moment, she had got past his secretary, and she heard his voice on the end of the line.

"Corliss?" Drew asked with surprise. "Something wrong?"

"Don't be silly. Can't I call up an old friend and invite him to lunch?"

"Are you serious?"

"Yes, I am."

"It's a good idea because I want to talk to you, too. How about the Rose Room?"

Corliss left the lab a few minutes past twelve. The hotel was within walking distance. The Rose Room was crowded, but Drew was already there, waiting. Seeing him here, in the city, in public, always gave her a start. He looked so neat and polished, so well dressed, so vitally professional.

"What did you want to talk to me about?" Corliss asked, after they had ordered. "Widow Huffman?"

"As a matter of fact, yes."

"Oh!"

"She's been around the neighborhood with an idea of restoring the old mill."

"A crazy idea!" Corliss corrected him. "I've heard about it."

Drew arched his brows with surprise. "You don't approve?"

"No."

"Why not? I thought it a good idea."

"Did you really? Or is it because Madeline Huffman thought of it? Who

156

does she think she is, waltzing into Willow Woods, wanting to take over, making a big splash—"

Drew frowned. "You really don't like outsiders, do you?"

She was instantly ashamed. She didn't know why Madeline Huffman annoyed her, she just did. "I'm sorry. That was rude and unforgivable."

"Johansen is asking a big price for the mill. Madeline's going to want the whole area to chip in, make it a community project."

Corliss sighed. "Well, you know how I love the old mill. I'd hate to see it disappear too, but if she spoils it, if they go in there and ruin the wonderful way it looks now—"

"Not change," Drew pointed out. "Preserve. There's a big difference. Madeline wants to have a party to raise money. A fancy affair at the Country Club. Twenty-five dollars a plate. Do you think it will go over?"

"It's as good a cause as any. I've been asked to donate to crazier things than

157

that!''

Drew smiled. "Good. Because the party's all set for Saturday night at the Country Club. Madeline will need some help. I want you to do all you can.''

"Is that why you wanted to see me? To ask me to help your Madeline with this idea of hers?''

He puffed at his pipe and eyed her. "You know everyone in Willow Woods. You're the logical choice.''

"I don't see how you figured that one out!''

"I know how you feel about the old mill. I thought if you were in on the bottom floor of this program, you could protect it, look after it.''

She stared at him. As usual, Drew made a lot of sense.

"I'm not sure. I'll have to give it some thought.''

"Now you're being stubborn and contrary.''

"I am not!'' she said angrily.

"Forget it. Eat!'' he said, tapping his pipe out into an ash tray.

"I'm not a child! You don't have to command me to do such things as eat."

Drew's big face flushed. Then he laughed. "Will you kindly just enjoy your food? How often do I buy you lunch?"

As quickly as she had become angry, she had forgiven him. "Not for a long time now. Not really since you used to come up to college to see me."

"That's right. So, please, be pleasant. Smile. Everyone will think I'm being mean to you."

"You used to come to the university to check on me for Father, didn't you? You never just came to see me for yourself."

Drew's gray eyes met hers. "You had to be watched. Every minute!"

She made another face and knew he was teasing. They went on to talk of other things. It only occurred to her later that he had avoided answering the question.

The next day, Corliss and her father received an engraved invitation to the party at the Country Club.

"Will you go, Father?" Corliss asked.

"I don't think I care to go out in public

just yet."

"But you're doing so well!"

"I don't want a setback, Corliss. I want to get back to the office one day soon."

Corliss received a phone call from Madeline Huffman that same evening.

"You know about the party, of course," Madeline said. "Drew told me you would help me. Could you come to the Country Club early Saturday? I'll need help with the seating."

Corliss took a deep breath. She wasn't by nature ungracious, and Drew had a point. If she was a part of the restoration drive, she could protect the old mill.

"When would you like me to be there?" Corliss asked.

"Could you come by six?" Madeline asked.

"Yes."

"Fine. I'm counting on you."

Perhaps Reese would come along too. It would be fun if Reese were with her. But when he heard about the arrangements, he shook his head.

"I can't be there that early. Not on

Saturday.''

"But, darling, you don't go to the office on Saturdays!''

"I have an appointment. Sorry.''

"Doing what?''

"The same old story. Business.''

"Oh, Reese!'' she sighed. "Sometimes I think you're just avoiding me!''

He laughed and pulled her close. "Come here and say that!'' He kissed her for a long moment. "Still think so?''

"No. But Burr's not being fair. He's taking too much of your time.''

"It won't be forever. I promise you that. Burr likes me. I'll be moving up in his organization soon.''

"You've told me that before, Reese, and it hasn't happened. I don't think I trust Burr.''

Reese kept his arms around her, and his green eyes looked down at her. "Forget Burr. Forget business. Forget everything – concentrate on me, will you?''

The night of the party at the Country Club, Corliss dressed early and arrived well before six. The Country Club house sat on the top of a high hill, overlooking Seabourne. Madeline had arranged for the place to be decorated with fresh flowers. The tables were attractive. Corliss had to admire the woman's taste.

"Oh, there you are, Corliss. I'm glad you're early. There's still so much to do," Madeline said. She had a sheaf of papers in her hand, and she began to review the guest list.

"You know everyone, Corliss. Goodness, I wouldn't want to seat someone with a party they don't like or cause any awkward situations. That's why I wanted you to help me. You know everyone—"

Together they went through the list, pairing off couples with other couples, putting around the place cards. Then suddenly, there was no time to think about anything else but the guests who came pouring in. Corliss watched for Reese. Why was he so late? Surely he would come any minute now.

"Hello, Miss Mitchell."

She was startled to find Burr Kaldner standing beside her. She smiled politely.

He was smoking his inevitable cigar, eyeing her with that way of his that put her nerves on edge. "Have Reese and Jennie arrived?" he asked.

Her heart gave a leap. Reese and Jennie? "No," she said carefully.

He looked at his watch. "Strange. They should have been here by now. I suppose Jennie insisted they stay horseback riding longer than they should have!"

"Horseback riding?" Corliss asked quickly.

"You know Jennie. Crazy about horses. Reese was taking her riding this afternoon. If they don't come within the next fifteen minutes, I'll get on the phone and find them!"

With that, Burr walked away, smoking his cigar. Corliss's heart had turned to ice. Reese had told her it was business that was keeping him busy today. Business! Did he call Jennie Kaldner business?

Corliss's head began to ache. Her eyes throbbed from trying to watch the door through the crowd. Where was Reese? What was keeping him? How could he come here with Jennie? How could he do that to her?

Then suddenly, she was aware of a commotion around the door. She heard excited voices.

"There's been an accident," someone said.

She caught sight of a police officer. She heard someone calling Burr Kaldner's name. Fear clawed at her, scratching along her nerves, bringing a quick, awful dryness to her throat.

"Officer —" she fought her way through the crowd.

Then Drew was there, blocking her way, his face grave.

She felt the room tilt. "Reese?" she asked. "Is it Reese?"

Drew nodded. "Reese and Jennie Kaldner. They've been taken to the hospital."

She clutched his arm for a moment, a chill going through her. Then she pushed through the crowd toward the door and ran out to her car. Drew was shouting behind her, but she didn't stop. Like a woman possessed, she started the motor, turned out of the driveway with a spin of the wheels, and went tearing down the road. Halfway down the hill, she saw flashing lights and a small cluster of people. The accident had happened here. She saw the twisted wreckage of Reese's car and her heart nearly stopped. Was Reese all right? Dear God, Reese had to be all right!

XII

The Country Club was just a short distance from Seabourne. But to Corliss it seemed like a thousand miles as she pushed her car as fast as she dared. Just ahead, she caught a glimpse of Burr Kaldner's fancy limousine. It seemed to her she hit every traffic light on red and spent agonizing minutes waiting for it to change.

At last the hospital! She had trouble finding a place to park. Her nerves were in shreds by the time she rushed inside to the desk in the lobby.

"Reese Sheridan," she gasped out. "Where is he? Is he all right?"

"The accident victim?"

"Yes. Yes!"

"You'll find him in emergency, miss. But I don't think—"

She didn't wait to hear any more. No

one could have stopped her. She ran down the hall. When she reached the door, she saw Burr Kaldner. Then at last she saw Reese, sitting in a chair outside one of the examining rooms, head in his hands.

"Reese!"

He was ashen, and there was a bandage on his forehead. His dark hair was mussed, and his green eyes were glittery with shock. But he was alive. Thank God, he was alive!

"Oh, Reese! Reese –"

She flung herself into his arms, and he held her. It seemed he was trembling from head to foot. He pressed his face against her hair.

"It's all right, Corliss. I'm not hurt. Just shaken up a little."

"I demand to know what happened!" Burr said with clenched fists. "I want to know whose fault it was!"

"Not mine, Burr," Reese said tiredly. "I've told you a half dozen times. The other car was coming down the hill on the wrong side of the center line. I had to swerve out of his way to avoid a head-on collision. We hit a utility pole, and my car spun around. The other car slammed into the passenger side.''

"Into Jennie. My Jennie!" Burr said, his voice going low and deep. Tears began to course down his cheeks. "My little Jennie, all broken and hurt—"

Corliss gripped Reese's hand. "How is Jennie, Reese? What's happened to her?"

"They're examining her now," Reese said in a voice that sounded as if he carried the weight of the world on his shoulders. "She was knocked unconscious. She was pinned in the wreckage. It took a little while to get her out—"

Reese couldn't go on. He lowered his head, covering his face with his hands.

"What's taking so long in there? Why won't they tell me anything?" Burr demanded.

He stomped up and down the hospital corridor, stopping nurses, demanding in a loud voice to be allowed inside the emergency room. Then at last the door opened, and Jennie was wheeled out, very pale, barely conscious.

"Baby," Burr said, bending over her. "Baby, are you all right?"

"Daddy—"

She closed her eyes as if too tired to talk. Burr stared at the orderly.

"How is she? What's happened to her?"

"We're taking her to her room. Three-oh-seven. The doctor will meet you there. You can talk to him."

Jennie was wheeled away. The three of them took the elevator to the third floor. Burr rushed out ahead of Reese and Corliss and straight into Jennie's room. Jennie was being settled, and after a moment the nurse chased Burr out. He stalked up and down the corridor. At last Dr. Rushley appeared. He was a young doctor, but a good one. Corliss had written many reports for him at the lab. Jennie was in good hands.

"Well, well?" Burr asked.

"Your daughter has had a back injury, Mr. Kaldner. It will affect her from the waist down. She's paralyzed."

Corliss turned away, suddenly ill,

biting her lip so hard she tasted blood. Reese had gone whiter still, and his eyes were like dark green holes in his head, burning with despair. Burr couldn't seem to move, and for once found no angry words to shout.

"It can't be true," Reese muttered. "It can't be true!"

"I'm afraid it is. We've already read the X rays. We have no reason to be hopeful," Dr. Rushley said.

"She was so happy going to the party," Reese murmured. "Like a child. All she talked about was who would be there and what they'd do and if I'd dance with her —" Reese's voice broke.

Corliss touched his sleeve. "Let me drive you home, Reese. You're in shock yourself."

"I should see Jennie first."

Dr. Rushley shook his head. "Just her father for now. Perhaps later she can have visitors."

Burr gave Reese one long, hard stare. His face looked bullish, his eyes shot steel, and then he turned on his heel and went into Jennie's room, closing the door after him.

"Come along, Reese. Let's go now," Corliss said.

They walked wordlessly down the hall, got in the elevator, and rode down to the lobby. They walked outside and got into her car.

"He blames me, Corliss," Reese said. "Burr blames me!"

"You said it wasn't your fault."

"It wasn't. But I was driving. I was the one that lost control. If I had kept the car from going into a spin, Jennie wouldn't be up there now . . ."

Corliss couldn't think of anything to say. She started the car and drove slowly to Reese's small bachelor apartment. Once they were inside, Reese collapsed in a chair, head back, eyes closed.

"Reese, are you certain you're all right?"

"Yes. Make some coffee, Corliss. Strong and black."

In Reese's tiny kitchen she started the coffee. Reese didn't want a light on in the living room. He sat in the dark. Corliss loosened his tie and helped him out of his jacket. When the coffee was ready, she gave him a cup and sat on a low footstool beside him.

"Burr worships that girl," he said slowly. "He has only one weak spot and that's Jennie."

"You must not torture yourself like this, Reese. It was an accident. You were not to blame."

"We were late. Perhaps I was driving a little too fast. It was my fault! It was, Corliss. It doesn't matter what anyone says," he said tiredly. "I'll always feel responsible."

Corliss got to her feet and took the coffee cups back to the kitchen. She found some aspirin in the bathroom and brought him two of them with a glass of water.

After he'd taken them, she made him stretch out on the couch. Leaning over him, she kissed him tenderly. But there was no response, no reaching out, no need to cling to her.

"Go home, Corliss. Please, just leave

me alone now. I have to think.''

She wanted to stay. She wanted to be with him, to comfort him, to ease his terrible guilt. But he didn't want her. He had asked her to go.

''All right. Phone me if there's any more news. Promise?''

''Yes.''

She closed the door behind her. It occurred to her that Reese hadn't told her about the afternoon, about going riding with Jennie. How many other times had there been that she knew nothing about?

Then she forced herself not to think such things. A sweet girl lay in the hospital, badly hurt. She felt deep sympathy and pity for Jennie. Besides, Reese loved her, Corliss, just as much as she loved him. Their love had endured many difficult times. It would endure this one.

XIII

Jennie Kaldner's condition was the talk of Seabourne for the next few days. Burr had called in specialists, but their diagnosis had been the same as Dr. Rushley's. Jennie would spend the rest of her days in a wheelchair. Reese was filled with remorse.

"You must stop blaming yourself, Reese," Corliss said.

"Tell me how, and I will," he replied.

She knew he spent a great deal of time visiting Jennie at the hospital.

"What else can I do?" he asked with despair in his voice. "I feel so sorry for her. I want to be kind."

"Yes. I understand."

There was such a gaunt, unhappy look about him. Burr had made a kind of peace with Reese, but it was an uneasy one. She knew she couldn't press Reese about the matter of Jennie. It was going to take time. Once again, she found that she must wait.

To push the worry of it all out of her head, to blot out the real situation, Corliss worked harder and harder at the lab. Paul seemed especially busy these days, and she knew he was impatient with Mitchell Electronics for being so slow in building Unit Two.

Paul was always at the lab ahead of her. Going down the hall one morning, she found him at his desk. "Good morning, Paul."

He lifted reddened eyes to her. "Is it that time?"

"Paul, didn't you go home last night?"

"Sure. For a little while. But I came back early. I think I'm on to something. But it's too soon to speculate. I hope, I mean – well, I do know one thing for certain. I got this in the mail yesterday."

He gave her a letter, and she read it with interest and surprise. "Paul, this is wonderful!" It was an invitation to speak at the Chicago medical convention in

September. "Oh, that's great! So you see, you're not nearly as unknown as you think."

"Perhaps not," he nodded. "I'm flattered. I'll hate leaving my work even for a few days, but on the other hand, how can I turn down an invitation like this?"

"You can't. Of course you can't!"

"No," Paul smiled. "Would you be able to stay late tonight and help me with some notes?"

"Elizabeth too? Frankly, Elizabeth is a little depressed these days. She needs to be occupied."

Paul lifted his head. He was not a handsome man. But attractive enough. There was something about his burning eyes and expressive hands that caught one's attention. "Alex Ward?" he asked.

Corliss was surprised. "I didn't know you knew about Elizabeth and Alex!"

Paul laughed. "Oh, you see, now and then I do get my head up out of the sand and see what else is going on in the world. If Elizabeth will stay, fine. Ask her to come back to my office, and I'll talk to her about it."

"You're a brick, Paul."

"Among other things," he said with a shrug of his shoulders that made them both laugh.

The morning work was heavy. Dozens of reports waited to be made, and the slides were carefully examined, the tests made and double-checked. Corliss found deep satisfaction in what she did here. During trying times, her work was a solace. During happy times, it was exciting and contenting. Often, she thought of Jennie Kaldner and always Reese was there in the back of her mind. If only there was some way she could help him now.

That evening, Paul suggested Corliss and Elizabeth take a long dinner hour before coming back to work. It was a hot, summer night. Elizabeth got behind the wheel of her car and suggested a drive before they ate. They left the main part of Seabourne and soon were going in the direction of the river. The water was cool, quiet. It flowed serenely and the willows along the banks were reflected in the water. Boats were everywhere. Lazy fishermen dotted the banks. It was a different world here. Like an oasis in the desert, this quiet little spot seemed unusual and refreshing in the busy city of Seabourne. Only Reese had never thought of it in this way. He'd hated it here.

Corliss rubbed her forehead, wishing she could keep Reese out of her thoughts. If only there was a way to break through to him. If only he would let her help him.

"Elizabeth, would you mind if I skipped eating? Would you just drop me off at Reese's apartment? I'll take a cab back or have Reese bring me."

"Things are no better between you two, are they?" Elizabeth said. "Well, do as you please."

Corliss had almost never dropped by Reese's place unannounced. But she knew if she phoned him, he would discourage her from coming. She went inside the apartment building and to Reese's door. It took him a moment to answer her ring.

"Corliss!"

"Hello, darling."

"What are you doing here?"

She stepped into the room. "I want to talk to you."

Reese looked as if he was getting ready to go out, and she saw flowers lying on a chair by the door. She picked them up and smelled them. "For Jennie?" she asked.

He nodded. "Yes."

"Reese –"

"You shouldn't have come, Corliss. I'm – I'm just not up to seeing you or talking about our plans or our future –"

She gripped his arms. "Reese, you can't let this ruin our lives."

"It's ruined Jennie's," he said miserably.

There seemed to be nothing she could say in the face of that. They stared at each other for a moment, and then Reese turned away.

"I need you," she said quietly. "I thought now, at a time like this, you would need me."

He faced her. "You have no idea how I need you."

"Then why –"

"Have I a right? Do I have a right to take so much from you when – when I don't deserve it?"

"Why are you always so hard on yourself?"

He shook his head. "Habit, I suppose. I've always had to be hard on myself. If I hadn't, I wouldn't be here now, I'd still be down there on the riverfront, running errands for Sadie. How do you think I got through school, through college, got this job with Burr? It wasn't by taking things easy. It wasn't by just getting by the best I could. I sweated blood for everything I got! You just never quite understood that, Corliss!"

"Oh, Reese, I did!"

"No," he shook his head. "Listen, Corliss, it's best if you go before we get into an argument. I'm not up to that, either."

"I only want to help."

He nodded. "I know, Corliss. Forgive me for being like this. Dear God, I do love you!"

He pulled her close for only a moment,

and then he broke away. He touched her cheek. "I have to go now, Corliss. I'm sorry. If I'd known you were coming—"

"You would have said not to come," she said sadly.

"Give it time."

"Time. It's always been time with us. Is it ever going to change?"

They left his apartment, wordlessly. They drove through the busy Seabourne streets, and he dropped her off at the lab. She leaned toward him and kissed him lightly on the lips. There was barely any response. Then with a wave, she watched him drive away. Feeling empty, rebuffed, hurt, she went inside, telling herself that the magic word was time.

They put in a hard session at the lab. It was ten when Paul sent them home. Corliss was tired, keyed up, alternately angry with Reese and then remorseful. As before, so many times in her life, she found herself thinking of Drew. He could always put things in perspective for her. She would talk to him about it. Tonight. Before she went home.

The sky had grown cloudy. Rain had been threatening for two days, and it was needed badly. At home, the lawn was showing patches of brown, despite Sam's tender care. The flowers had withered, and the rosebushes were suffering.

Willow Woods seemed very dark and still as she turned the car down the narrow roads. The air was stifling. Not a leaf was stirring. It was as if she were driving into a deep, dark green tunnel. Never before had the woods seemed frightening. Perhaps because her nerves were jagged, she was aware that she was gripping the wheel tightly.

An abrupt flash of lightning nearly blinded her. The thunder was like an angry rumble. A few fat drops of rain fell. Then the rain came down in earnest. She started the wiper blades. Driving slowly, she reached Drew's house at last. She was relieved to see the lights burning there.

She pulled into the driveway. What was that? She put the brakes on quickly. Was it someone clad in a dark raincoat, slipping away around the corner of the house?

Had it only been Mrs. Petrie? She couldn't be sure. She sat in the car, uneasy, uncertain. The wiper blades made a rhythmical sound. There was no one in sight now. Could she have imagined it?

Still, she was afraid to get out of the car. She pressed the horn, blowing it repeatedly until at last the door opened and Drew stood in the wedge of light.

"What is it?" he shouted.

She ran from the car through the rain and stepped into Drew's house, gripping his arm. "There was someone out there! Someone in a raincoat. I thought it might be Mrs. Petrie. But I'm not sure. It frightened me."

"Mrs. Petrie went to bed hours ago! With a headache."

"Are you sure?"

Drew laughed and closed the door. "I'm sure. Now, what brings you?"

"Let me catch my breath first."

"You're shaking like a leaf!"

"It was spooky coming through the woods with the storm starting, and then seeing someone slipping away through the rain. Aren't you going out and look around?''

Drew frowned. "Chances are, whoever it was is gone now."

"Could it have been Mrs. Petrie?"

Drew sighed. He dropped an arm around her shoulder. It was solid and comforting. "Would it make you feel any better if I wake her and convince you that she hasn't left her room?"

"At the risk of sounding ridiculous, yes!"

"All right. I'll only be a moment. Go into the den. There's a pitcher of iced tea. Have some. I'll be back in a minute. Brush the rain out of your hair and relax. Get hold of yourself."

When he took his arm away, she felt frightened again. But the den was cozy. She took solace in the familiar room, despite the lightning that ripped the sky so fiercely beyond the glass doors and the wind that twisted the branches of the trees. She rubbed her arms, feeling cold.

In a few moments, Drew was back. Mrs. Petrie was with him, fully dressed.

Her hair was wet. Behind her glasses, her eyes were owlish.

"I've solved our mystery. Mrs. Petrie heard the rain start and went to rescue a potted plant or two, fearing they'd be blown over and broken. That's all."

"Sorry if I gave you a fright, dearie," Mrs. Petrie said.

"It's all right. With everyone skittish about the prowler in the woods, you understand—"

"Yes, of course," Mrs. Petrie said. "Will that be all, Drew?"

"Yes. Sorry I disturbed you."

Mrs. Petrie left.

"Satisfied now?" Drew said.

"No. Her hair was so wet. And her shoes. Didn't you notice her shoes? She had mud on them. There is no mud on your concrete driveway!"

Drew studied her for a moment. A clap of thunder rumbled across the room. He went to pull the curtains across the glass doors. Suddenly, the storm was blocked out. Even the thunder and lightning seemed muted.

He poured her a glass of iced tea and set it at her elbow. "I'll remember what you said. That's immaterial now. Something's brought you here at this time of night, through a storm. What is it?"

"Reese."

"Oh."

Drew frowned and tasted his tea. He waited for her to speak.

"Ever since the accident, he's been so strange. Different."

"Guilty?"

"Yes. Guilty. He seems bent on putting himself through the wringer because of the accident."

"I think I can appreciate his feelings," Drew said. "How is the Kaldner girl?"

"They're giving her some therapy at the hospital, but what good can it really do?"

"This is something Reese has to work out for himself, Corliss," Drew said. "Give the man time."

"It seems so long already!"

Drew laughed. "Always the impatient one."

She managed a smile. Perhaps she was impatient. She didn't mean to be. But she knew Drew was level-headed. He always made sense. And if he thought so –

"It will work out if it's supposed to, Corliss."

"That's your philosophy of life, isn't it?"

Drew lifted his big shoulders in a shrug. "I suppose it is at that. By the way, I've news about your father."

"Father?"

"Yes. I tested him. I gave him a brief I'd drawn up for a new contract, with a doubtful clause in it. Just to see if he'd catch it. He did. I got my ears chewed good for it!"

She laughed. "I'm glad to hear it."

"He's coming along physically and mentally. I won't be surprised to see him back at the office soon. Before you know it, everything will be back to normal. Reese, too."

"You really think so?"

"Yes. Then you can fly the coop."

"Wouldn't you be glad to have me out

of your hair, once and for all?'' she asked.

Drew lifted his iced tea glass in a salute. "Immensely relieved. After ten years of looking out for you, what else could I feel?''

"Ten years!'' she murmured. "I was just a teenager when you first came to Willow Woods as Father's company attorney.''

"You were all legs, big eyes, and impossible ideas.''

"Gee, thanks.''

They laughed together, remembering.

"How did it happen?'' she wondered. "How did it come about that you decided you had to look out for me?''

Drew shrugged. "I hate to see kittens go astray or little girls fall down and snub their noses. I have this streak in me. Paternal, I suppose.''

She scoffed. "Paternal! I think you just liked to be bossy.''

He picked up a magazine and hurled it at her. In retaliation, she began to fling small sofa cushions at him, and in a moment he was chasing her around the room, shouting at her as she laughed and dodged him. At last he caught up with her, big arms pinning her tight. His gray eyes were flashing.

"For that, brat, I think you're going to get a paddling to end all paddlings!"

"You lay a hand on me, Drew Fielding, and you're going to be sorry!"

She reached up and nipped his ear with her teeth. He yelled in exaggerated pain. Then she rumpled his hair and made a face at him. He gripped her by the shoulders. He shook her gently. For a moment their gazes locked, and abruptly, he let her go. He moved away to the desk.

"You'd better go home. It's getting late."

"Kicking me out?" she asked, and her throat felt tight.

"Bedtime for all puppies, kittens, and little girls," he said, and there was a slight smile on his lips.

"Or maybe you have a rendezvous with Madeline Huffman," she retorted.

He stared at her. For a moment, he seemed about to say something.

"Drew, who is she?"

He shrugged. "Just someone who moved to Willow Woods. I don't know why everyone is in such a stew about her!"

"Tch, tch. You're awfully edgy all of a sudden."

"Run along," he said tiredly. "Your father must be wondering where you are."

There seemed nothing left to say. She picked up her purse. The rain had stopped. With luck, she'd find the stars beginning to shine when she went back outside.

Drew watched Corliss until she had reached the car and drove away. Then he stepped out for a moment to breathe deeply of the rain-drenched air. It was sweet and clean, and the dark clouds were already rolling away, and the skies were clear.

The phone rang. He was tempted not to answer. He was in no mood for anything but standing here, staring at the stars. But at last, he turned away and went inside. The voice was low, quiet, seductive. He rubbed a hand over his forehead.

"Hello, Madeline."

"The storm's over."

"Yes," he said. "Did you call me just to tell me that?"

"No. Could I see you? Would you be able to drop by?"

"What's the problem?"

"We need more money for the mill. The Country Club dinner netted a nice amount, but not nearly enough. I need suggestions. I also need the name of a good architect."

"Madeline—"

"Don't make me beg, Drew. I'm not good at that."

There were a dozen excuses he could offer, but he knew she could see through them all. "All right, Madeline. Give me a few minutes. If you promise to make it brief."

She laughed and said goodbye. The line went dead. Drew replaced the phone in the cradle thoughtfully.

Half an hour later, he was driving the short distance to Madeline's house. It blazed with lights. At the slam of his door, she appeared at the window, waving to him.

She was a lovely woman. Well put together, with silky blonde hair and luminous eyes. He paused long enough to light his pipe. Somewhere a dog barked, and the storm had left the quiet so deep he thought he could hear the cars on the highway three miles away.

"Come in, Drew," Madeline called.

She wasn't as tall as Corliss or as graceful. But she had her own good points and knew what they were. There was always a certain scent about her. She had expressive hands. A quiet laugh. A face that at times mirrored shadowy things in her past.

"Hello, darling," Madeline said.

He braced himself. Then her arms were around him, and her lips were against his, warm, sweet.

"Remember how it was, Drew? Remember?" she asked. "I know you haven't forgotten. Tell me you haven't!"

XIV

Madeline Huffman had appointed a committee to attend to the matters of the restoration of the old mill. Drew dropped by Corliss's house one evening to tell her that she was a member.

"They've decided to look the place over with an architect and see what has to be done. You're to meet with the others at the mill Saturday morning at ten."

"Who put me on this committee?"

Drew grinned. "I did."

Corliss wasn't happy with the idea of it, and yet in a way, she was glad to have something to occupy her mind. Reese was still so withdrawn. So distant. They hadn't gone out since Jennie's accident. She kept reminding herself to take Drew's advice and be patient. It would be a mistake to press Reese again. He was not a man who liked to be pushed into any kind of corner, even by her.

Saturday morning, Corliss decided to walk to the mill, despite the promise of a very warm day. She wanted to go early. In truth, she wanted to pay a sentimental visit before the others arrived.

The woods always fascinated her in the morning, cool, shadowy, smelling of green leaves and moss. She walked quietly in her sneakers, her hair tied back with a bright ribbon. As she approached the mill, catching a glimpse of the deep pool, the graying shingles of the roof, the huge, motionless wheel, she paused. Memories were everywhere here. Memories of Reese, herself, and all those good golden days of the past.

She was glad to see that no one else was there. It had been ages since she had been inside the old mill. She decided to step in and look around. Sunlight filtered through the dusty windows. Someone had been here. Perhaps people on a picnic. The litter they'd left behind disgusted her.

What was that? She heard a strange noise. Suddenly the shadows of the mill seemed sinister. Her heart was in her mouth. Footsteps!

"Who's there?" she called out. "Where are you?"

Everything became very still. Everything but her thumping heart. If it was one of the committee members, they would call out. But there was only a strange silence.

"Who's there?" she called again.

There was a room at the rear of the mill, once used for storage. She decided to have a look. Just as she approached it, she heard another sound directly behind her. She spun about, a scream about to come tearing out of her mouth. A man stood there, tall and thin, with a dark line of moustache above his lip – the same man she had seen in the road. He stared at her for only a second, and before she could get her wits about her, he was gone. For a moment, she was too stunned to move. Then she rushed to the window and peered out. But she could see no one. Hear nothing. Had she imagined it? No! He had been here, just as he had been there that morning on the Willow Woods road.

"Anyone here?"

Corliss jumped, startled, and then relaxed. It was only Madeline Huffman.

"In here," Corliss called.

Madeline came to find her and looked around with lifted brows. "This is a real mess, isn't it?"

"Madeline, did you see anyone as you came in?"

"Why, no."

"Someone was in here. He ran when he saw me. It looks as if he's been living here!"

"Oh, dear. A vagrant?"

"I don't think this man was a vagrant. He was too well dressed. I've seen him before. Once on the road. In fact, I nearly ran him down."

"Oh, dear, should we stay here?" Madeline asked. "I wish the others would come!"

"I keep thinking about the prowler."

"So do I. Strange—"

They heard sounds of others arriving, and for the moment Corliss pushed her fears into the back of her mind. There was business to take care of, all kinds of suggestions to listen to, and a few arguments on how to spend money on the restoration. Some wanted to make it a showplace. Others wanted to hold down the expense as much as possible and do something about beautifying the grounds around the mill.

"Let's keep it as it is. Old, rustic, lovely," Corliss argued. "Isn't that the idea? To restore? Not to change?"

There were murmurs of agreement.

The architect tramped about, measured, prodded, poked, and said little, but promised to give them a full estimate of costs at their next meeting.

At last, they were free to go.

It was a very warm Saturday. Often, in the summertime, Reese took her to Henderson Lake a few miles from Seabourne. It was a popular spot. The thought of the cool water, the sandy beach, the fun of a boat – she longed to go. As soon as she reached the house, she phoned Reese at his apartment.

"I've got a wonderful idea," she told Reese. "Let's go to the lake. I'll fix a picnic lunch if you like."

He hesitated, and her hopes began to fade all over again. "Not today, Corliss. Or tonight either."

What could she say to him? How could she reach him? "Reese, you can't do this to yourself. You can't let this eat away –"

"Please, Corliss –"

She knew it was pointless to continue. He would only get angry and make the situation all the more unbearable. "How is Jennie?"

"She went home yesterday. The therapy the hospital gave her didn't really help. She appreciated the gift you sent."

"It was a small enough thing to do. I honestly wish it were more."

"I know," Reese sighed. "Well, why don't you ask Elizabeth to go with you? Have a good time for me."

"But Reese –"

"Please. Have fun."

"All right, darling. If that's what you

want."

They said goodbye and hung up. She thought about it for a moment and then decided to phone Elizabeth.

Corliss left her father lazing in a lawn chair, content to read. She gathered her bathing things and drove away. Elizabeth was ready and waiting. It was a forty-minute drive to Henderson Lake, and the highway was busy. Elizabeth talked a great deal about Paul Gilman and the lab.

"You and Paul have become friendly lately, haven't you?"

Elizabeth made a face. "Not like that."

"Does that mean it's still Alex?"

Elizabeth turned her head away, and her hands were suddenly clenched together in her lap. "God help me, yes."

Corliss had to bite her tongue to keep from saying anything more. They rode on in silence. When they reached the lake, they saw it was jammed. Every available boat had already been rented.

"It looks like the beach for us," Corliss said.

"I haven't been swimming in ages. Not since –"

"I remember. The last time we were here, Alex brought you, and I was with Reese –"

They changed in the bathhouse and ran across the scorching sand in their bare feet, heading for the wide, blue expanse of inviting water. Corliss waded in and began to swim, Elizabeth keeping pace. It was good to concentrate on the motion of arms and legs, to conquer the water, to swim until the tiredness began to set in. She tried not to think of Reese or Jennie Kaldner or what had happened. Today, she was going to let the sun soak away all her cares and worries. At last, they started swimming back to the shore. Splashing and dripping, they waded out.

"Hello! I thought I recognized you two mermaids!"

Alex Ward stood there, attractive in swimming trunks, his big shoulders marvelously tanned. Elizabeth's smile was frozen. It seemed no place for Corliss.

"I think I'll have a cold soda," Corliss

said. "Could I bring you one, Elizabeth? Alex?"

"Don't bother," Alex replied. "I've got a beach umbrella and a cooler full of drinks over there. Come and join me. Come along. Both of you."

Elizabeth didn't seem to be putting up much of a fight. There was nothing to do but go.

"I didn't realize you spent weekends around Seabourne, Alex," Corliss said.

"Seldom do. This is an exception. I kept thinking about the lake, and since I have to be in Seabourne Monday on business, I said to myself, 'Alex, old boy, why not treat yourself right?' So, here I am."

"Don't you get tired of traveling? Don't you want to settle down to one place?" Corliss asked.

Alex shook his head. "Not me! No desk job for me. I like to move around. I want action!"

"Just the opposite of Paul," Corliss said, flashing Elizabeth a quick look.

"Paul Gilman? He'll turn into a test tube," Alex scoffed. "By the way, how's that fancy equipment he was building? Did he finish it?"

"No," Corliss said. "Not yet."

"What's the delay?"

"It's at the other end of things. At the plant," Elizabeth replied.

"I see. I supposed by now that Gilman had got a patent and was having it manufactured and that he was a millionaire!"

"Stop teasing!" Elizabeth laughed.

Alex leaned toward Elizabeth and kissed her. Corliss turned away and closed her eyes, suddenly feeling very lonely.

"Come to dinner with me tonight, Elizabeth," Alex was saying. "We'll have a great time."

Corliss sensed Elizabeth was looking at her but didn't return the glance.

They spent a lazy day at the beach. Alex seemed bent on entertaining them. But Corliss felt like a fifth wheel. She spent most of her time in the water or strolling the beach, feeling lonelier than she had felt in a very long time. If only Reese were with her. If only —

It was about four when Corliss and Elizabeth left the lake. It was a silent ride back to Seabourne. Corliss dropped Elizabeth off at her apartment.

"You think it's a mistake for me to go out with Alex, don't you, Corliss?" Elizabeth asked.

Corliss reached over and patted her hands. "It's your affair, honey. Your heart. I just don't want to see you hurt again."

"I think I can handle it this time."

Elizabeth waved goodbye, and Corliss drove back to Willow Woods. She decided to drop in on Drew. Fuzz was lying languidly under a tree and didn't bark as she called to him.

"Lazy dog," she laughed, ruffling his fur.

The house seemed quiet. She let herself in through the glass doors on the patio.

"Anyone home?"

No answer. She walked quietly through the house looking for Mrs. Petrie. She pushed open the door to the kitchen. Mrs. Petrie had not heard her. She was busy packing a small basket with assorted canned foods.

Corliss was about to call to her, when Mrs. Petrie reached deep into a cupboard and brought out a pistol. Corliss was so surprised that she stepped back out of sight. Leaving the door ajar, she watched Mrs. Petrie tuck the pistol into the basket. Then she snatched it up and hurried away, slipping out the back door.

XV

After Mrs. Petrie had gone, Corliss went to find Drew. But he was nowhere about, and she discovered his car wasn't in the garage. She was about to go when she heard him coming. She went to meet him. He was dressed casually, but there was a briefcase under his arm. He looked tired and angry.

Drew was never surprised to see her, but today his smile was brief.

"What is it?" she asked.

"Business problems."

"Tell me."

"Promise not to pass it on to your father?"

She wrestled the briefcase from under his arm and laughed. "You know I'm not a tattletale. What's wrong? Why are you working on a Saturday afternoon?"

Drew went into the den, Corliss following. He paused long enough to light his pipe. "It's Tom Whittier. I've heard rumors I don't like."

"Gambling again?"

"I hear he's up to his neck in debt. I've warned him about it. But the real problem is Paul's piece of equipment."

"What do you mean?"

"I think Tom's stalling, and I have no idea why."

"Paul's so anxious to get the equipment built!"

"I know. I have another goody. I heard Burr's after the Wagner contract, too. If we lose out this time —"

Corliss heard the depression in his voice and laughed to cheer him.

"How would you like to visit Sadie's Place?" Drew said.

Corliss looked at him with surprise. "I've only been there a time or two with Reese, and . . . Well, sure, I'd love to go!"

"Fine. I'll pick you up about eight . . . Don't tell your father any of this. Just say we're going for a drive."

Corliss didn't linger long at Drew's place. He seemed preoccupied and was itching to get at the papers in his briefcase. She decided not to tell him about Mrs. Petrie. She would wait until later when the time was right.

At home, she had dinner on the patio with her father. When he heard she was going out with Drew, he seemed pleased. Drew came by right on time. They drove away in companionable silence. When they passed Madeline Huffman's place, Corliss gave it a quick glance. The house was dark.

"Madeline's not home."

"It doesn't appear so," Drew replied.

"Is that why you asked me to go to Sadie's?"

"Don't be ridiculous."

They talked no more about Madeline Huffman, although Corliss wanted to ask many questions. She just wasn't sure she wanted to hear the answers.

Seabourne was busy, noisy, hot. But when they drove toward the river and

Sadie's Place, the air grew cooler. There were plenty of cars, and the sound of the jukebox came blaring out to them.

"Why do people like it here?" Corliss asked.

"I think it's Sadie they really like. She's straightforward and honest. Tolerates no nonsense. Then, of course, those card games in the back room . . ."

"I didn't know you came here!"

"I don't very often. But I handled a legal matter for Sadie once. In connection with the company. Her husband worked for Mitchell Electronics some years ago, and he died on the job. There was an insurance hassle, and I got in on the act."

"Pro or con?"

"Pro," Drew grinned. "Which didn't make me a choice friend of our insurance company. But Sadie deserved the settlement. Joe had worked for your father more than twenty-five years."

"And the insurance payment set her up in business?"

"Yes."

Tall trees surrounded the place. The

river flowed gently downward. Even with the jukebox sounding, there was a serenity about Sadie's Place. It was not the typical night spot, all plush and hustle-bustle. Their steps echoed across the porch. The screen door slammed shut softly behind them. Drew paused, taking her arm.

Sadie saw them immediately. "Well, as I live and breathe! Drew Fielding! What brings you and your girl here?"

"Not my girl," Drew said quickly. "Just an old friend."

Drew turned back to Sadie. "Do you have a quiet table, Sadie? I'd like to talk to you."

Sadie eyed him, hands on her ample hips, head cocked. "Now, you're sounding like a lawyer. Come this way. I've got a spot that is just right."

The table was blocked from public view, half hidden in a small hallway. Sadie motioned for them to sit down. Then she leaned her elbow on the table and cradled her chin in her cupped hand, listening and waiting.

Drew filled his pipe first.

Sadie held the match for him, smiling. "Always liked a man who smoked a pipe."

"I'll get right to the point, Sadie. It's about Tom Whittier."

Sadie leaned back. She fingered her orange hair and then laced her gaudy beads around her hand. "Okay. What about him?"

"He's deep in debt. Gambling. Who's got a hook into him?"

"That's none of your business or mine."

"It might mean his job, Sadie. I don't want to fire the man. I want to help him, if I can. But he won't level with me."

Sadie thought about that for a minute. Then she nodded. "You've always been straight with me, Drew. Okay. Tom's in up to his eyeballs. To a man called Cassiday. A stranger in town."

"Cassiday?"

"Yeah. Tom owed Cassiday about five hundred. Then Tom wanted to try and win it back. Now, it's up to a thousand."

Drew pursed his lips. "That's a lot of money to a young engineer like Tom."

"I reckon it is."

"How's it going tonight?"

Sadie shook her head. "Not good. Cassiday's a sharper."

Drew puffed at his pipe for a moment. "Why is Cassiday willing to continue the game when Tom can't pay up?"

Sadie got to her feet. Someone was calling to her. She shook her head. "That's one I can't figure. Looks like Cassiday wants Tom under his thumb for some reason."

"Who is this Cassiday?"

"Don't know. Not for sure. Just got an idea," Sadie said.

"Care to pass it on?"

"No. Listen, I got to run. If you hang around long enough, maybe you'll get a look at Cassiday yourself."

Sadie hurried away. Drew looked across the table to Corliss. "Shall we wait?"

"Why not?"

"I'll order us something cold to drink."

The place fascinated Corliss. She'd never understood why Reese liked to come here. But now, perhaps she did. It was unique. Different. Mostly men frequented the place. It must give Reese a sense of pride to know that once he had lived in this area, which was not considered the best in Seabourne, and that he had risen above it. Reese had always been so determined. He was going to be somebody. He had vowed that when she had first known him as a boy. It was something he had never forgotten. It was coming true. Only she wished it hadn't been Burr Kaldner that had helped make it possible.

"Want to dance?" Drew asked.

"But I'm not your girl."

Drew flushed. Then he reached out a hand. "Just keeping the record straight. Come on. You haven't danced with me in years!"

"Not so," Corliss said. "I danced with you last Christmas holiday."

Dancing with Drew always came as a surprise. He moved so lightly and easily over the floor for a big man. But then

Drew was always surprising her some way.

The music was loud and a little corny. The dance floor was very tiny. Only one other couple was dancing. Drew held her lightly, and after a time, Corliss dropped her head to his shoulder. It was such a comfortable, friendly shoulder. His chin brushed across her hair. There was something hypnotic about the music, the smoky room, the dim lights, the babble of voices. It was another world here. One she did not know. But it was all right as long as Drew's arms were around her.

The music stopped.

"Put in another quarter," she said. "Please."

They went on dancing, saying very little.

"Who taught you to dance?" she wondered. "Some college co-ed?"

"No."

"Who then?"

"A woman I knew."

"Now we're getting down to the nitty-gritty. Who was she?"

He gave her a grin. "My aunt."

"I don't believe you."

"You know I lived with my Aunt Tracy before I came to Seabourne and Willow Woods. Aunt Tracy raised me, put me through college. She did many things for me, including teaching me to dance!"

"I wish I could have known her."

"You would have loved her," Drew said. "She died before I came here, and I still miss her."

Corliss dropped her head on his shoulder again. She thought of Reese. She wondered where he was and what he was doing. He probably had gone to see Jennie. Or was he busy with Burr? She only knew he had not wanted to go out tonight, that he hadn't bothered to give her a real explanation.

Suddenly she was aware of a commotion. They stopped dancing. The sound of loud voices was coming from the back room. With a look of determination on her face, Sadie made for the door, marching with rigid shoulders.

"I'd better see what's going on," Drew

said. "Stay here."

Drew followed Sadie into the back room. The loud voices continued, and there was a shattering crash of furniture being broken. Then at last it grew quiet. Three men came out, followed by Drew and Tom Whittier. Tom had a bloody nose.

"What happened?" Corliss asked. "Are you all right, Tom?"

"Sure, I'm just fine! Cassiday worked me over before Drew and Sadie got there."

Corliss gave Tom a handkerchief to hold to his bleeding nose. Out of the corner of her eyes, Corliss saw a tall, dark man slipping away.

"Is that Cassiday?" Corliss pointed urgently.

"One and the same," Tom nodded.

"Drew, that's the man I saw in the middle of the road that day! The man I found hanging around the old mill!"

"Are you positive?"

But Cassiday had gone.

"Tom, you'd better go on home now,"

Drew said. "We'll talk Monday morning."

Tom's eyes flashed. "No. I won't be there. I've got a way out of this whole mess. Burr Kaldner will bail me out, give me a job—"

Drew straightened. It was one of the few times Corliss could remember seeing him truly angry. "You hire on with Burr," he shouted, "and I'll take you apart. I mean it, Tom. Report to my office Monday. We'll settle it then."

Tom hung his head. "Okay. Okay. I'll be there."

"Go on home," Drew said, more gently. "Get some sleep."

Corliss and Drew left a few minutes later.

"Drew, do you think Cassiday could be the prowler that's been around Willow Woods?" Corliss asked.

"It's possible, I suppose. But just because you see a man in the road and at the mill doesn't make him a criminal, Corliss."

"Now you're making fun of me!"

"Just trying to be objective."

"If he's not guilty about something, why does he act the way he does?"

"Maybe he's a bit eccentric," Drew said.

"Well, then, while we're on the subject of eccentrics, what about Mrs. Petrie?"

"You don't like my housekeeper, do you?"

"I think she's peculiar, that's all. Why would she pack a basket of food and slip a pistol into it as well?"

"What's this?" Drew asked quickly.

Corliss repeated what she had seen. Drew shook his head.

"I don't understand, but I'm sure there is a logical explanation."

"I admire your faith and trust in the woman," Corliss said wryly.

"I'm a lawyer, remember? Everyone is innocent until proven guilty."

"Then I won't worry about it anymore. I've told you. I've done my duty."

"I'll do a little investigating."

They drove on through the night, and when they reached Corliss's house, it was dark.

"Do you realize you haven't mentioned Reese once this evening?" Drew asked. "Are things any better?"

"No."

They were silent for a moment, and Corliss was struck, as she had been several times, by the tragedy of it all. In a few split seconds, so many lives had been touched and changed.

"It's late. I'd better go in," Corliss said.

Drew gripped her by the shoulder with a big hand. "Goodnight, brat."

Corliss laughed and leaned toward him, brushing his lips with hers. He drew back with surprise. Then still laughing, she got out of the car and waved goodbye.

In a moment, he drove away, driving a little faster than usual. She went inside. She wondered if Reese might have phoned. But she checked the pad of paper by the phone. Martha had left no message. She was disappointed but not surprised.

It took a while to fall to sleep. Then it seemed she had barely closed her eyes when she awakened with a start. Something was rattling against her windows! She sat up, hand at her throat. Who was there?

"Corliss! It's me. Reese. Wake up. I have to talk to you!"

XVI

It took Drew a bare five minutes to reach his house after leaving Corliss. A light burned inside. Mrs. Petrie was up. He frowned, remembering what Corliss had told him about his housekeeper. Granted, Mrs. Petrie was a little odd, but what on earth would she be doing with a pistol? Then there were those other times Corliss felt she had seen Mrs. Petrie acting suspiciously.

He was still frowning as he went inside. Mrs. Petrie was in the kitchen, drinking hot tea, her frizzy hair sprouting in all directions around her head.

"Oh, it's you," she said.

"Who were you expecting?" Drew asked quickly.

Mrs. Petrie gave him her pixie grin. "Oh, maybe some of the Little People."

Drew laughed. "Do you really believe

in such things?''

"Me mother did, bless her," Mrs. Petrie said.

"I've got a question. I want you to answer me honestly, Mrs. Petrie."

The woman was instantly on guard. "What's bothering you, Drew?"

"What do you know about a basket of food and a pistol?"

Mrs. Petrie eyed him. The woman had great composure. He had seen none to equal it except in the courtroom.

"Oh, that," she said with a shrug. "I took old Mr. Millard the last of the blackberries. He's interested in antiques, and he asked to see the pistol. It was my father's, you know."

"I didn't know you and Mr. Millard were such good friends."

Mrs. Petrie shrugged. "He's just an old man. Lonely. Shouldn't be living alone. Speaking of which, that widow's been phoning you, every hour on the hour." Mrs. Petrie sipped her tea with a haughty air. "That Widow Huffman. Said you were to call her back, it was important, no matter what the hour.''

Drew nodded thoughtfully. He believed the woman was lying, but he couldn't be sure. It disturbed him. Perhaps he hated the uncertainty more than anything else. He went to the den to make the call to Madeline. It took her only a moment to answer.

''Oh, Drew, at last! I thought you'd never phone.''

''What is it?''

''Drew, it's so lonely here.''

''I told you it would be when you came to Willow Woods, remember?''

''Don't be cruel.''

''I'm not.''

''Please come. Even if it's only for an hour.''

''Madeline—''

''I know I'm shameless. I know I shouldn't beg. But Drew, darling, I need you.''

He closed his eyes for a moment and rubbed his forehead with a shaking forefinger. ''All right,'' he said. ''I'll come.''

He hung up. For a moment, he wondered if he'd taken leave of his senses. Why egg her on? Why let her play her little games? Hadn't he learned his lesson once? Was it necessary to learn it again?

Madeline had a phobia about the dark. Every light in the place was burning. He parked the car in the drive and walked quickly toward the door. She'd heard him. She was waiting.

"Drew—"

He stepped into the room and straight into her arms. She clung to him, and after a moment, with a sigh, he put his arms around her.

"Madeline, this has to stop."

"Why?"

"You know why. Perhaps you don't care about your reputation, but I care about mine. There isn't a soul in the Woods that doesn't know I'm seeing you."

Madeline laughed with a toss of her blonde hair. "What does it matter?"

"It matters," he said quietly, taking her arms from around his neck.

"It didn't matter once what anyone thought. Only we mattered."

"That was a long time ago."

"And I was foolish. I let you go."

Drew moved deeper into the room. Madeline had furnished the house with her usual good taste. Her things were expensive, thanks to the money her late husband had left her.

"Aren't you going to say anything?"

"What is there to say?" he asked.

"That you still love me, that you've never forgotten me. I want to hear that more than anything else in the world."

Drew fumbled for his pipe. Somehow, he couldn't get used to the idea of her saying such things so frankly. Once, when he was young and foolish, he had longed to hear them. He had never wanted to give up hope that she would eventually be his. Then Charles Huffman had come along with his money and prestige, and Madeline had taken only one look to know he represented what she wanted. There would be no waiting. Huffman was older, already established. He'd inherited some money as well as made a pile of his own. In comparison, Drew had seemed like what he was. A struggling law student with high ideals, and no funds, and a long, long way to go.

"It's too late, Madeline," he said.

"I don't believe that."

"Have you forgotten, Madeline? Do you think I could forget how you turned away from me – so easily, so quickly?"

"You're still angry."

"What did you expect?"

Madeline laced her pretty hands together. She sat down near a lamp that caught all the beauty of her hair. She looked at him with tears on her eyelashes.

"I was young. Foolish. I didn't know what I was throwing away. Oh, I had a decent life with Charles. But it lacked something very vital. It lacked excitement. Ardor. Passion. Do you understand?"

She came to him again. Her arms were around him, and as always, he was aware of her perfume. Her lips were there, waiting. Almost against his will, he leaned down. Her kiss was so warm, so eager.

"Darling, darling, darling," she murmured. "I still love you so. Darling —"

Corliss was awake now. Peering out the window, she couldn't believe that it was Reese. He had never come like this before, so late, so obviously upset.

She pulled on her slippers and searched for the prettiest robe she had in the closet. She ran a comb through her hair and then walked quietly through the sleeping house. She unlocked the doors to the patio and stepped out. Reese was there, smoking, his cigarette glowing red in the dark. She turned on a dim patio light and saw that his eyes were stark, his face gaunt.

"Reese, what is it? What's wrong? Why are you here so late?" She went to kneel beside him, and for a moment he took her face into his lean hands.

"Corliss, I have to talk to you. It couldn't wait until morning." He seemed to be struggling for the right words.

He got to his feet and turned away, keeping his back to her. She knew from the hard outline of his shoulders that something was very wrong. She knew him too well. Going up behind him, she slipped her arms around is waist and pressed her face against the familiar hollow between his shoulder blades.

"I love you, Reese. I'm glad you've come. No matter what it is! At last, you've come to me."

"Don't say that," he said harshly. "Please, don't say that!"

"Darling, you're my life, my love, the very beat of my heart—"

With an abrupt movement, he crushed her into his arms, and his kiss was so hard and intense that her lips felt bruised. Then he let her go and stepped away from her.

"I want you to believe something. That I love you. That I will always love you, Corliss. I promised you there would be a time for us. I meant that. You have to believe I meant that!"

She stared at him, an unnamed fear creeping into her heart. His green eyes were burning.

"Reese—"

"Don't hate me for it. Whatever you do, don't despise me. It can't be helped. This is something I feel honor-bound to do."

"Reese, you're not making any sense. No sense at all!"

He stared at her, and in that brief moment, she was aware of the night as if it was commanding her to remember every detail, as if this was something that must be burned in her memory. There were stars shining and a slight breeze bringing the scent of roses from the flower garden. An insect sang, a prediction by all the old legends that it was only six weeks until frost. She remembered thinking, "Where has the summer gone? Why, it's only begun!"

Then Reese spoke again. The night was suddenly black, and all the stars were gone. His voice cut down to stone reality, to bitter truths.

"Corliss, next week I'm going to marry Jennie."

XVII

Corliss felt as if the world tipped and then came to a grinding halt. Only moments ago, everything had seemed dark. Now there were spears of light stabbing her eyes, bright greens and yellows and spots of red. She groped for something to lean against and felt the coldness of the patio table.

This couldn't be happening! She was having a nightmare. Wake up, she kept telling herself. Wake up! This isn't true. I'm having a bad dream. Wake up!

Then as if in slow motion, she saw Reese lift a hand as if to touch her and then let it fall back to his side. He was here. He had said those awful words!

"Jennie loves me, Corliss," Reese said. "All this time, she has loved me. What else can I do?"

"But you love me," she said, finding

her voice at last. "I love you! We were going to be married. As soon as possible. You can't do this. You can't!"

"But I am doing it," he said tonelessly. "Corliss, what can I say? How can I make you understand?"

She stared out into the dark night. The locust was still calling. Six weeks to frost. The summer was gone. Why was she thinking about such unrelated things?

"I'm responsible for the accident," Reese said.

"You're not!"

"But I feel I am. I have to do this, Corliss. Say you don't hate me for it. Please, tell me that?"

She couldn't speak. She couldn't seem to orient herself to this night and what was happening. Reese took a step toward her. His hands gripped her shoulders. His green eyes seemed to devour her. Hunger rippled across his face. He bent his head to kiss her again, and she wrenched away from him, suddenly unable to bear it a moment longer.

"Don't touch me. Don't ever touch me

again!"

She ran. Across the patio and into the safe darkness of the house. She hid there behind the patio doors, watching him. In a moment, he turned away. Soon she heard the sound of his car starting, the whisper of tires across the drive and out to the lane. Then he was gone, the motor roaring with a sudden, angry burst of acceleration. Gone. Like dust settling, like clouds blowing away, like stars falling. Gone!

She stumbled down the hall to her room and flung herself across the bed. She wanted to cry. She needed the luxury of tears. She wanted to scream. To be hysterical. But she found she could do none of these things. She was wooden. Dead. Used up. Incomplete. Bleeding. She was being crushed inch by inch. Heartbeat by heartbeat.

At last, she sat in a chair by the window. The stars were still there. The trees. The locust. The world had not changed after all. Only she had changed. And Reese –

The tears came at last. She had never

cried as much or as hard before. When they were gone at last, she was spent. She dressed, crept out of the house, and struck out through the woods, not knowing where she was going or even caring. There was a heavy dew. Her shoes were soon soaked. Wet branches slapped her in the face, and she stumbled on paths that had once been familiar, but now she was too stunned to know or remember anything but Reese's voice saying, "I'm marrying Jennie!"

"Little Jennie Kaldner," Corliss murmured. "In love with Reese. Jennie in a wheelchair, Jennie and Reese—"

She walked until dawn. She found that she had come back to the mill. She knew she would have to come here at last, It had all begun here. It was fitting that it should also end here.

"Give me your hand," Reese had said on that golden yesterday in that other world. "I'll help you. We'll climb up high. Dive. We'll touch the bottom. Can you open your eyes under water?"

"No."

"I'll show you how. I'll teach you.

Come on, Corliss. Hurry up. Don't be afraid. I've got hold of your hand. I won't let you fall.''

But he had! He had let her come crashing back to earth, broken into a million pieces! Reese was gone. He would never come back. Reese was gone! There would be no time for them after all. It was lost. Over. Finished.

And I'm dying of it, she thought with anguish. I'm dying!

She watched the mist curl above the murky water for a little while, stared at the old weathered boards of the mill, the huge wheel. She would not come here again. She would not help Madeline Huffman. She would resign from the restoration committee. How could she bear to come here now?

She hurried away at last, nearly running, a ragged breath tearing at her throat. Until she heard Fuzz barking a greeting, she did not realize where she was. Then she saw Drew's gate and went to lean on it. It was ridiculously early. Just past dawn. Sunday morning.

She failed to speak to the dog, and he continued barking loudly, circling her happily, wanting to play. It roused Drew. In a moment, he was at the glass doors of his den, hair rumpled, knotting the belt of his robe. "Corliss? What on earth?"

He came across the wet grass to her, unmindful of his slippers, telling Fuzz to be quiet. She looked at him with hollow eyes, and he knew that somehow, some way, everything had stopped for her.

"What is it?"

She didn't think she could say the words. But somehow she forced them past her dry lips. "Reese is marrying Jennie Kaldner."

"My God!" Drew said in a hushed voice.

She covered her face with her hands and heard a strange whimper that she knew had come from herself. Drew put his arm around her, and she felt her knees give way beneath her. Then he picked her up in his big arms and carried her inside. The sofa was soft and comfortable. She was suddenly aware that she was extremely tired. Drew bent over her and brushed back her hair with a gentle hand.

"Rest, Corliss. Things will look brighter when you wake up."

"How can they?"

"Life goes on. You'll find that it does."

She reached up to touch his face. "Dear Drew. Always here when I need you."

He smiled at her. "Try to sleep. I'll be right here beside you. You're not going to let this get the best of you, Corliss. You've got too much Mitchell in you. I won't let this ruin your life!"

She slept then. From sheer exhaustion. Strange how the human mind knew how to rest itself, how to draw back in sleep and pull its resources together. When she awakened, the sun was streaming in the window. A tray waited beside her, and there was a pot of coffee, some of Mrs. Petrie's muffins, and Drew at his desk, watching her.

"Better now?" he asked.

"I don't know."

"Go wash your face. Splash some cold water in your eyes. Then come back and have breakfast with me. I hate eating alone. Run along. I'll phone your house so they won't be alarmed.''

''Will you tell Father?''

''Yes, I'll tell him.''

''He'll be glad,'' she said wearily. ''He'll be relieved.''

The cold water refreshed her. The coffee gave her substance, and Drew's presence was comforting.

''Better now?'' he asked.

''Yes. Thank you, Drew.''

''I'll see you home.''

''No. Please. I'd rather go alone.''

''All right.''

She took a few minutes to stop and stroke Fuzz's head and to speak with him. He looked at her with his faithful eyes and seemed to sense there was something wrong. He rubbed against her legs as if his devotion could ease her pain.

She walked home through the mocking sunlight, through green trees, and down narrow footpaths. Father was waiting for her on the terrace. When he saw her, he got to his feet and came to meet her. She noticed that for the first time, he wasn't using his cane.

"Corliss –" He put an arm around her shoulder, and they walked to the house together. "I'm sorry," he said. "But we won't discuss it. Not now. Unless you choose."

"I don't want to talk about it ever!"

"Have you had breakfast?"

"Drew fed me."

"Ah, yes. I was thinking. Perhaps we should take a trip together. Abroad. Or to the West Coast. Wherever you'd like to go. It might be good for us both."

"It won't do any good to run away, Father. It will be the same when I come home."

He nodded. "All right. I suppose it's best. There will be difficult days ahead. Embarrassing days. But you'll endure, Corliss. You're made of good metal."

That afternoon, Corliss went to tell Elizabeth what had happened. Elizabeth accepted the news calmly, but her white face told Corliss how badly she felt. "What can I say, Corliss? I know how shattered you must be."

"Since that very first day I saw Reese, he has been important to me. I never for a moment thought there would be a time like this—"

"It must not be easy for him either, Corliss," Elizabeth pointed out. "Marrying a woman simply because he feels obligated."

Corliss rubbed her aching head. "I wonder if that's all there really is to it. He'd been seeing Jennie. I know that. Even before the accident."

"But Jennie was the boss's daughter. That's different—"

"You're being sweet and kind, as usual," Corliss said.

"You're hurt, terribly hurt, but no matter what he's done, you still love him, don't you?"

Corliss nodded slowly. "Loving Reese has been a part of me so long. How can I stop now?"

The next few days went just as her father had predicted. The word got around town very rapidly, and the formal announcement of Reese's wedding to Jennie was in Monday's papers. People glanced at her and then looked quickly away. Everyone felt sorry for her. The woman shunned. Jilted.

Only Elizabeth stayed the same. She made an effort to keep the days normal in every way. Paul too, more or less ignored the news. They concentrated on lab work. Reports. Tests. Analyses. They kept things humming, and Paul worked them hard, often keeping them after hours. On the day of Reese's wedding to Jennie, Paul invited Corliss and Elizabeth to dinner, something he had never done before.

"I have to get out once in a while," Paul said with a smile. "Just to see if the world is still there."

Paul did his best to make the evening enjoyable. He talked more than Corliss had ever known him to talk before. His rather dry stories were balanced with Elizabeth's more cheerful ones. They kept Corliss out late, and somehow she got through that day, and the next, and the next.

It was about a week later that she heard more about Reese. Drew dropped by one evening to tell her.

"It's all around town, Corliss. Reese has been made vice-president of Kaldner Enterprises."

She lifted her head. "Oh!"

"So, that's why he married Jennie Kaldner," her father said bluntly.

"I don't believe that!" Corliss said angrily. "I know you both believe it, but I don't. He wouldn't do something like that just to be vice-president!"

Drew turned away, pipe clenched between his teeth. For a moment, the air was charged in the room. Corliss twisted her hands together. It couldn't be true. Reese wouldn't have married Jennie just to advance himself. He wouldn't be that cold, that calculating!

"Anyway," Drew said, "Burr didn't get the Wagner contract. We settled it today."

Father smiled broadly. "Good. Good! Burr's got a few things to learn. He can't ride roughshod over everyone."

"This brings us up even again," Drew said. "If Tom Whittier would just get Gilman's test equipment ready, we might have something good going."

"What about Tom?" Father asked.

"He sold his car to meet his gambling debts. I hope he's learned his lesson. But I'm not sure about him —"

"Give him the benefit of the doubt," Father said. "He's a brilliant young man. I don't want Burr Kaldner to snatch him away."

"Brilliant in one way," Drew said. "Quite stupid in another. If he could leave the cards alone —"

"When will Paul's equipment be ready?" Corliss asked. "I know he wants to announce it in Chicago when he goes to the medical convention next month."

"It won't be ready by then, I'm afraid."

The phone interrupted. It was Madeline Huffman.

"I need your help with the mill, Corliss," she began.

Even thinking about Roberts Mill was a wrench to Corliss's heart. She couldn't bear to work on the restoration project now, to be forced to talk about it, look at it, examine it, watch the progress being made.

"I'm sorry, Madeline. I'm afraid I'll have to resign from the committee."

"Oh, you must stay with us, Corliss! It's so important. I thought the old mill was special to you."

The tears were stinging her eyes. Once, it had been. Now, it was only an echo of painful memories.

"I've been collecting donations. There are only a few people in Willow Woods that I have not contacted. Let's see, there's Mrs. Johnson, the Simpsons, and Mr. Millard. If you could just see one or two of these people, Corliss, it would be such a help," Madeline said.

Corliss thought of a dozen excuses, but Madeline kept talking, persuading, insistent. There was no way to put her off.

"All right," Corliss said at last. "I'll see the Simpsons – and Mr. Millard, if he's there."

"Fine. Thank you so much. I'll set up a meeting for next week, and see you then."

Corliss made no promise about attending the meeting, but said a quick goodbye and hung up. She disliked asking people for contributions. But the next day, Saturday, she decided to get it over with. The sooner the better.

The Simpsons had heard about the restoration program and were enthusiastic. They gave Corliss a substantial check.

The Millard house had a closed, vacant look. Curtains were drawn. She rang the bell anyway, to be sure. She heard something inside. But no one came to the door. That was odd.

She knocked at the door and called out. "Mr. Millard, are you there? It's Corliss Mitchell."

There was no answer. Only silence. But she'd been so certain she'd heard something inside!

Corliss hurried back to the car and drove away, suddenly very anxious to see the familiar sight of home.

XVIII

Behind Sadie's Place there was a large cottonwood tree. Two men were there, dark silhouettes in the night.

"All right, what is it you want with me? Why did you want to meet me here?"

"You seem to be an enterprising man." The laugh was quick and coarse.

"Say, you're really sharp, mister."

"There's a lot of money at stake."

"Keep talking."

"How are you at opening safes?"

"What is it you want? Spell it out."

"Interested?"

"Depends. I'm here sort of incognito, if you know what I mean."

"It figures."

"Who's been talking? Sadie? She been shootin' off her mouth or is it someone else?"

"Relax, I just took a shot in the dark.

You a professional?"

"I'm professional enough," came the reply. "Tell me what you want."

"The Gilman Laboratories. There's a safe in the office behind a picture. Open it, get out a cardboard tube that has some drawings in it. I want to borrow them for a few hours."

A light flared. Cigar smoke drifted on the night air.

"How much is in it for me? What are the drawings?"

"A new piece of lab equipment. Five thousand for you. A bonus if you leave town the next day."

"Skip the bonus. I intend to stay right here in Seabourne. I like it here."

"A long way from New York."

"What do you know about New York, mister?"

"Or is it Chicago? You don't belong here, and I know it. Well, is it a deal?"

There was a moment of silence.

"All right. A deal. When do I hit the place? Where do I bring the drawings? Back here to Sadie's Place?"

"Don't be a fool. You'll hit the place tonight. There's a motel on Cherry Street. The Windward. Know it?"

"That dump? Sure, I know it."

"I'll be there. Room fourteen. It's around to the rear. Be there by midnight or our deal is off."

"When do I get paid?"

"A couple of hundred now to prove I mean business. The rest when you finish."

The two men shook hands.

Paul Gilman had done the unprecedented twice. First he had taken Elizabeth and Corliss out to dinner the day Reese Sheridan married Jennie Kaldner. He had done it at Elizabeth's insistence. "To help her through the day," as Elizabeth said.

Paul was surprised how warm he suddenly felt about Elizabeth Lane. Odd. She had worked for him some time now, and he thought of her as a competent lab technician and not much more. She was a steady worker. Plodding almost. Whereas Corliss had imagination and drive. Corliss would be good in research, and sometime

246

soon, he might begin to channel her efforts more in that area.

The evening with the two girls had been pleasant. A diversion. He found himself wanting to repeat it, only this time just with Elizabeth. So he had asked her, and she had agreed, surprised but receptive.

It was odd to be forty-eight years old and going out on a date, nearly as eager and excited as a teenager. There hadn't been time for romance in his life. He had neither needed it nor wanted it. The lab and his work had been enough. More than enough.

Elizabeth answered his ring, and he stepped into her apartment. He looked around, interested. Everything had a soft, feminine look, from the flowered furniture to the vase on the mantel to the frilly curtains. It came as a kind of jolt after the place where he lived, which had the bare necessities and not much else.

"I made a pitcher of a certain concoction I stir up in the summertime," Elizabeth said. "Would you like some before we go?"

"Why not?"

So he sat uncomfortably on the soft divan, listening to Chopin on Elizabeth's record player, and polished his glasses twice. His tie felt as if it were choking him, and rubbing his cheek, he wasn't certain he'd got the closest shave possible. His beard was always annoyingly heavy and black.

Elizabeth returned, two glasses in her hands. She was a tall, pretty woman with brown hair and the gentlest of eyes. Her cool fingers brushed his as she handed him the glass.

"Here you are. Don't try to analyze it. It's impossible," she laughed. "I'll only tell you there is the juice of lemons, oranges, a dash of cherry, some tea, and a very special spice. There is the secret. The spice!"

He sipped it and found it surprisingly good. "It's delicious, Elizabeth."

"You're in a coffee rut," she smiled. "All the time, drinking coffee!"

He leaned forward, nodding. "That's right I am in a rut. I admit it."

Elizabeth smiled. "You're so nice, Paul. It's a shame to bury yourself as you do in the lab. Oh, I know it's important, what you're doing there. But . . ."

Paul frowned and set the drink aside. "If only Tom Whittier would hurry up with that equipment!"

"Still no progress?"

"Very little. I'm about ready to give Drew Fielding an ultimatum. Produce or else—"

"You wouldn't go to Burr Kaldner? I doubt he'd have an engineer that could do the work, to begin with, and secondly—"

Paul smiled. "I don't like the man either. Do you know he approached me about it? He wouldn't say where he'd heard the news of it. That worries me a little. But I turned him down."

Elizabeth seemed relieved. "I'm glad you did!"

"There are other places. Other men to build it. All I have to do is find them. If Whittier doesn't produce soon—"

Elizabeth sat down beside him. "What about Unit One?"

"It's built. I did it myself. The two units must work together."

"But I've never seen a model of it!"

"No," Paul shook his head. "I have it under lock and key at the bank. When Whittier gets his unit done, I'll get out mine and hook them together."

"You make it all sound very important."

"I've been more than four years perfecting the plans, Elizabeth. It can mean a big step forward in blood analysis, cut off many precious minutes of time and in some cases, hours. Think what it can mean in an emergency, in research, in the hospitals – perhaps in time, a small working model of it can be used in doctors' offices –" He broke off, realizing he was getting carried away. He'd thought about the equipment so much, it was as much a part of him as breathing. "I'm sorry, Elizabeth."

"Don't be. I think it's all very exciting."

He finished his drink and got to his feet. "Let's find some dinner somewhere that will be just as exciting. Where would you like to go?''

"The Oaks would be nice. Or the Rose Room. Or we could get some delicatessen food and have a picnic. A weiner roast? Seafood over at the Wharf in Jonestown. Anywhere.''

He smiled. ''It doesn't matter to me. You're the one. Please, choose.''

"The Oaks.''

It was an evening he would always remember. Elizabeth was lovely by the candlelight on their table. She suited the place. There was a certain elegance at The Oaks, good service, good food. He found he was enjoying himself, and when it came time to see Elizabeth home, he was almost sorry.

At her door, she gave him her hand. He ignored it. Reaching for her, he kissed her clumsily, awkwardly. He bumped his glasses in doing so and they were askew on his face. She laughed and straightened them for him.

''Elizabeth, I want to see you again.''
''Paul—''

There was a withdrawn look on her face. She wanted to be kind. But she didn't want to see him again on this basis. "Don't you think it best? Since I work for you –"

"That doesn't matter."

"Paul, I'm sorry."

A dry taste came to his mouth, one of old disappointments, old loneliness. "I see. It's Alex Ward, isn't it?"

She didn't answer. She didn't need to. He said a quick goodnight and hurried away from her door. Driving home, he decided to drop by the lab. It was a safe world there. He knew where he was going and why. It had been a mistake to stray.

It was late. Well past midnight. He turned on a light in the lab, took off his jacket, and flipped open a notebook of notes. Soon he was picking up a pencil, putting a slide under the microscope, checking the material in a batch of test tubes in the refrigerator, and inspecting others he had subjected to heat. He noticed something. Perhaps, just perhaps, it was significant. Soon he was

252

deep in his work.

It was about three o'clock when he realized how tired he was. There was a couch in his office. He stretched out with a sigh and was instantly asleep. He was dreaming. Someone was in the room with him. He smelled cigar smoke. He fought to open his eyes. There were footsteps hurrying away. He sat up with a start. "Who's there!"

Running steps now! The opening of the back door! He tore after them, sliding down the hall, colliding with a waste basket, spilling outside. But all was dark. There was only light traffic in the street. He could hear no one, see no one. He had no idea which direction to go. It was pointless. Whoever it was, had gone. He went back inside. The lab was in order. Nothing seemed out of place.

With a nervous hand, he flipped on the lights in his office. There was nothing. But the picture hiding the safe was slightly crooked. Had he left it like that?

"No!" he murmured. "No!"

Like a wild man, he tore away the picture. The safe was closed. Locked. He twirled the dial and opened it. With shaking hands, he took out the tube of drawings and pulled them out. He spread them on his desk. All of it was there. He knew them by heart. Even the slight smudge of ink in the right hand corner was his. He began to feel relieved. He had only dreamed it. Just a bad dream.

Then he saw something that chilled him to the bone. Holding the drawings to the light, he saw the heavy indentations. Someone had traced every line!

He felt sick. Shaken. Then someone had stolen the drawings, copied them, and then replaced them! And like a fool, he had been in the room when the thief had returned them. Asleep!

He reached for the phone.

The police arrived ten minutes later. The report was made. An inspection of the lab revealed nothing. They dusted for prints but found what they suspected would only be his own.

"It's the work of a professional, Mr.

Gilman," the police officer said, sounding worried. "This isn't an easy safe to open. Someone knows his business. I didn't know we had anyone in Seabourne that professional. A few petty thieves, perhaps, but no one that could open a safe without blowing it, or smart enough to leave no clues —

Paul clenched his fists. "You've got to find him! Don't you understand? My plans have been stolen!"

"See a lawyer, Mr. Gilman. Get a patent on this stolen material as quickly as possible. That's my advice to you. That will offer you protection —"

Paul breathed deeply. "I suppose it's possible. Thank you. I will see a lawyer."

He thought of Drew Fielding. But Drew was connected with Mitchell Electronics. Whom could he trust? Wouldn't Mitchell Electronics profit if they could get both units built and in operation? Without him? There was no patent. He had no real proof the work was solely his own.

He wiped his sleeve across his forehead. He would have to make plans. Perhaps go directly to the patent office in Washington and see what to do. As quickly as he could.

"It's not my night," he thought wearily. "First Elizabeth won't see me, and now this—"

It didn't seem odd to him that he had placed Elizabeth first in his mind.

XIX

When Corliss went to work at the lab the next day, she learned what had happened. Paul was badly upset, and the entire business did nothing for Corliss's already shattered nerves.

"I'll be going to Washington on the four o'clock plane this afternoon. I want you to take charge while I'm away, Corliss," Paul said.

"Of course. And good luck, Paul."

"I'm going to need it!"

Corliss welcomed the extra work. Anything to keep Reese out of her mind. When she wept long hours at night, she told herself it was fatigue, nerves. When she came to the lab every day and stayed late every night, she convinced herself that it was because there was so much work to be done. If she was fooling no one but herself, she didn't really care.

Paul returned on Friday afternoon, looking tired and worried. "It didn't go very well. So much red tape! But I think I've got the ball rolling."

The pace at the lab didn't let up. Paul shifted more and more of the work to Corliss and Elizabeth. Sometimes, Corliss barely stopped for lunch. And when she did, she chose small places nearby, places where she and Reese had never gone together. Her favorite was just two blocks away, a plain little café. She felt comfortable there. No memories lurked in the shadows.

She was not hungry these days. But she ate a sandwich and drank some hot tea. She was nearly finished when she was aware that someone had paused beside her table. She looked up.

"Hello, Corliss."

She was stunned. Her throat went as dry as paper, and those stabs of light were in her eyes again.

"May I join you?" Reese asked.

"No. I'm just leaving."

"Corliss, I must talk to you!"

"No!"

"Please."

All the numbed and dead senses inside her came instantly to life. She ached with the sight of him, with all the familiar things she remembered that were so dear to her. The black hair, the green eyes, the way he looked in his clothes, the flash of white teeth, and more than anything, the hunger she saw in his eyes and the line of his mouth. She shook her head and began to grope in her purse for money to pay her check.

He put his hand over hers. "Wait."

"Don't touch me. Don't ever touch me!"

He took his hand away as if he had been burned. A wave of anguish passed over his face, and in that moment, she knew how unhappy he was. She felt sudden pity for him.

"How is . . . your wife?" she asked.

Then the tip of his tongue went across his lips. "Jennie's not too well."

"I'm sorry to hear that. Truly."

Reese nodded.

Corliss got to her feet. She must escape him. Now. This minute. She hurried away and left the check with too much money, not wanting to wait for her change. She rushed out. Then she nearly ran all the way back to the safety of the lab. This must not happen again! Not until she could bear the sight of him. She could not endure another unexpected meeting or hear the plea in his voice.

The meeting intruded on her thoughts for the rest of the afternoon and made concentration hard. She was relieved when it was time to go home. Alex Ward stopped by for Elizabeth. He was definitely back in Elizabeth's life again and had been dating her steadily. Alex came into the lab to wait for Elizabeth to clear her desk for the day.

"You girls awe me," Alex said with a laugh. "You look so terribly industrious and important."

"Oh, we are!" Elizabeth said.

"If you're ready, pet, let's be on our way," Alex said.

"Ready. Where are we going?"

"Anywhere your heart desires."

Elizabeth laughed and linked her arm through his. "Wherever you are, that's where my heart is."

Alex kissed her lightly. "That's my girl."

Corliss left the lab. Driving home, she thought again of Mr. Millard and the donation she was to try and collect for restoration of the mill. She decided to stop by his house on her way home. If she didn't, Madeline Huffman would be phoning about it again.

Willow Woods seemed cool and shadowy after the hot day in the city. The summer was nearly gone. Soon the heat would be going out of the sun, the leaves would begin to turn, and Willow Woods would be blazing with color. There was no lovelier place in the autumn.

Mr. Millard's house still had a closed, empty look. She decided to try the bell, just in case. She pressed it and could hear it ringing inside. But there was no sound this time. Millard was still away.

On second thought, she decided to go

around to the rear of the house. Sometimes the old fellow worked in his garden or a small workshop where at one time he had refinished furniture as a hobby.

"Mr. Millard! Are you here?" she called.

No answer. But the door to the workshop stood ajar. That was odd. Surely he would have locked it if he were away. She pushed at the door, and it swung open. She stepped inside and paused, the shop dimly lighted.

"Mr. Millard! Are you here?"

She heard a sound. Fear clawed at her throat. Why had she decided to come here alone when she suspected before that there might be something strange about the place?"

Somehow, drawn by curiosity and morbid dread, she stepped deeper into the workshop. Suddenly, she was aware of movement behind her. She spun about, but something came crashing down on her head, and stunned, she caught a foggy glimpse of a man, and then there was only blackness.

Corliss gradually became aware of someone slapping her face. She struggled to open her eyes. Drew was bending over her.

"Corliss. Corliss!"

She tried to sit up and found she was a little dizzy.

"What happened?" Drew asked anxiously. "I was on my way home and saw your car here. The house looked closed and I wondered—"

"I came to see Mr. Millard. I was looking for him, and I stepped into the workshop. Someone hit me. A man—"

"Are you all right?"

"I think so."

"Should I take you to a doctor?"

"No. I've just got a lump on the head, that's all. I'm all right now."

"But who did it? Why?"

"I don't know. The other day I came here, and I thought I heard someone inside the house, only no one came to the door."

"It looks as if Millard has been away for some time," Drew said. "That's odd. Mrs. Petrie said she had brought him some of the blackberries and an old antique pistol for him to see. The pistol you saw her putting in the basket that day—"

"And you believed her?" Corliss snapped.

Drew helped her to her feet. For a moment, the world tipped and then slowly righted itself.

"Can you drive, Corliss?"

"Yes. I'll be all right."

"I'll follow you home."

She had a splitting headache, and it was an effort to concentrate on her driving, but she made it home safely. Drew went on with a wave of his hand.

She decided not to tell her father about the incident. It was foolish to upset him needlessly. She would let Drew handle it. She was almost positive that the man called Cassiday had been staying at the old mill. Then with so many people around, he had been forced to move. So perhaps he was in Millard's house that first time she'd stopped—Had it been Cassiday in the shed just now?

There were so many questions. And no answers.

Corliss spent a quiet evening at home, nursing her headache. It was late when the phone rang by her bed. She froze. Her heart stopped beating. She knew the voice instantly.

"Corliss, don't hang up on me. Please. Talk to me!"

Before she could hear any more, before she could be tempted to listen, she slammed up the receiver. Was it going to be like this? Was Reese going to plague her? If he continued, how long could she hold out against him? Right this minute, she wanted to call him back, hear his voice, talk with him. But she couldn't. Reese was no longer free. She had no right. How could she both hate and love him at the same time? Hate him for what he had done to her, love him as she had loved him for so many years?

When the phone rang again a few minutes later, she nearly didn't answer it. But it rang persistently until she snatched it up. Drew was calling this time.

"I've had a little chat with Mrs. Petrie. She tells me that when she went to see Mr. Millard that day, he wasn't home. She still claims it was blackberries she was taking him."

"I know it wasn't, Drew."

"We won't make an issue of it now. Not just yet. Anyway, I notified the sheriff. He made a thorough search of Millard's place. No one was there."

"Cassiday," Corliss murmured. "It sounds just like Cassiday! First you see him and then you don't! If I'd only gotten a better look at the man. But it was shadowy in the workshop—"

"I know Willow Woods as well as anyone. I'm going to look around on the weekend. If Cassiday's hiding here, I'll flush him out, Corliss."

But Drew had no luck. He dropped by on Sunday to tell her.

"What about Mrs. Petrie?"

Drew frowned. "I'm keeping an eye on her too. Now, don't worry, Corliss. If Cassiday is playing hide-and-seek with you, we're going to catch him!"

September came to Willow Woods. The air was cool in the mornings and often a fog hugged the ground. The trees were turning, giving a hint of what the autumn would bring. Sam Worth's flower garden was at its peak, and she had never seen it lovelier. She was reminded that soon Indian summer would come and go, then autumn and winter would set in. She tried not to think about the winter without Reese.

A rash of flu struck Seabourne. The lab was busier than usual because of it. Then one day Paul came in late, looking very pale and ill.

"Paul!" Elizabeth said with alarm. "You've caught the flu!"

"I'm afraid so. Just keep your distance, girls. I've got a few things to do and then I'm going back home to bed."

He had been in his office only five minutes when he asked Corliss to join him. She knew the medical convention in Chicago was Wednesday. Paul was to deliver his papers at that time.

"I've arranged for Doctor Williams from Milwaukee to give my speech, Corliss. I can't go. I'm just not up to it. Even if I shake the bug in the next forty-eight hours, I'll never be able to make it. The notes are all prepared. I'd like for you to take them to Chicago, meet with Doctor Williams, and review them with him. Could you do that?"

"But Paul—"

He gave her a weary smile. "You can do it, Corliss. You know the material nearly as well as I do. It would be a great favor to me and an enormous help to Doctor Williams."

"What a shame that you can't deliver the speech yourself!"

"It's the way the old ball bounces. I'll still get credit for the paper. Now, will you go?"

"How can I refuse?"

As it was, the trip to Chicago came as a welcome relief. It was good to pack her things, get aboard the plane, and leave Willow Woods and Seabourne behind. She would arrive at noon, meet with Dr.

Williams, and come home the next day. Paul had arranged for her to sit in on some of the speeches, especially those concerning research, and she was looking forward to it.

But more than anything, she found she was glad to be free of the thought of Reese for a few hours. Every time the phone rang now, she feared it was going to be him. Every time she went into a store or a café in Seabourne, or even walked down the busy streets, she feared she would see him.

How much could she take? When her heart yearned for him so much?

Her plane landed at O'Hare on time, and as quickly as she could, she caught a cab to her hotel. She had taken Paul's reservation, and as soon as she reached her room, she phoned Dr. Williams. They arranged to meet in the hotel coffee shop. There, over coffee, she reviewed the notes with him.

"These are very interesting, Miss Mitchell. Paul's done some great work here!"

"We think so too."

"It's an honor for me to deliver the speech for him. I hope you'll tell him that, Miss Mitchell."

When Corliss had finished with her business, she found an hour for shopping, picking up little gifts for Elizabeth, Paul and her father. She saw an outrageously shaped pipe and thought of Drew. With a laugh, she purchased it and tucked it into her purse.

Dr. Williams had been kind enough to invite her to dinner with some of his colleagues, but she had refused. She didn't exactly relish having dinner alone, but she was in no mood for strangers. Room service would suffice. She spent a few minutes staring out her window. The hotel overlooked Lake Michigan, and the view was spectacular. Someone knocked at her door. Perhaps Dr. Williams had thought of more questions. She unlocked the door, keeping the chain in place.

"Hello, Corliss."

The strength went out of her. The fight. The determination never to see him again. But he was here! In Chicago. Where no one knew them. Where no one would see them together.

"Reese, what are you doing here?"

"It's a business trip," he said. "But I won't lie to you. I timed it with yours. You're not going to turn me away now, are you? I must talk with you, Corliss. I must be with you. Please."

She reached up and took the chain off and opened the door wider. He stepped inside.

XX

The room suddenly seemed too small, airless. Reese looked at Corliss and gave her a smile.

"Why have you done this?" Corliss demanded.

"What's wrong with two old friends meeting?"

"Everything."

"Have dinner with me somewhere."

"No, Reese. The answer is still no."

"Well, then, we'll have it here."

She shook her head. "I said no, Reese. I meant it."

"The coffee shop downstairs?" he persisted. "Out in the open. In public, where everyone can see us? How can you object to that?"

"It's wrong, Reese!"

He sighed deeply. "I must talk to you. Give me a few minutes, that's all I'm

272

asking."

"Is it?"

"I won't touch you."

"All right," she said finally. "I'll go to dinner with you. As long as you understand –"

He nodded solemnly. "I understand. Shall we go now?"

"Yes." She walked out of the room ahead of him. Silently, they went down the hall to the elevator. The convention had filled the hotel with doctors. She hoped she would not see Dr. Williams.

The coffee shop was full, and a line was waiting.

"This is no good," Reese frowned. "I know of a quiet little club. It's early. We could have the place to ourselves. It will be easier to talk."

He took her arm to propel her through the crowd. His fingers seemed to burn her flesh. They had difficulty getting a cab. A few minutes later, they were riding along Lake Shore Drive, and Reese talked of the weather and his flight. She listened, hands twisted tightly together in her lap.

As Reese had predicted, the supper club wasn't busy. But it was dimly and romantically lighted with candles on the table and music playing softly. Another time, this would have been a delight to them both.

Reese ordered for them, and when the waiter had gone, his green eyes searched hers. "I've thought about something like this ever since –"

"Reese, you promised!"

"I know I have no right. But I have to tell you how it is. I want you to know about Jennie –"

Corliss closed her eyes. "I don't want to hear about your wife."

Jennie's a good person. Burr worships her. She's not well. The accident has weakened her considerably. She's so frail –" Reese paused to rub his fingers over his forehead. "I do what I can to make her comfortable and happy. I try to be kind even when – when I don't love her."

"Reese, don't say these things to me. Please –"

He raised his head, and his eyes were

burning with loneliness. "I must say them to someone. You have a right to know. I took your happiness and threw it away for Jennie—"

"Jennie? Or yourself?"

Reese was startled. He stared at her. "What do you mean?"

"You're vice-president now."

"That was Burr's idea. Not mine! I think he only did it to please Jennie. He would do anything for that girl!"

"What am I supposed to do about it?"

Reese's eyes flickered. "Nothing," he murmured. "Only say you don't hate me. That you have tried to understand."

"I don't want to talk about it, Reese. It was a mistake to come here. You should never have done this. I want to go back to my hotel. Now."

The waiter brought their food. Reese smiled at her. "You may as well eat, hadn't you?"

He had won again. So she forced the food between her lips. She didn't enjoy any of it. She felt guilty and angry with herself. How did it look? Out in a place like this, with a married man she was once engaged to? If someone who knew them were to see them, what would they think? The worst, of course. This was wrong, wrong, wrong! Reese tried to make her linger. He suggested a dessert and more coffee. She refused both. "If you won't take me back, I'll go alone," she said.

He nodded. "All right. We'll go."

They took a cab back to the hotel. Traffic was heavy. There were senseless delays. The meter kept running, ticking away the time. It seemed forever before she saw the hotel. Reese paid the fare and walked with her inside. He insisted on seeing her to her room. At her door, he unlocked it for her and pressed the key into her hand.

"May I come in?"

"No. This is goodbye, Reese."

He tightened his lips. For a moment, he stretched out a hand to touch her face and then withdrew. She ached to go into his arms, to be held, to be kissed. With tears blurring her vision, she turned away. But he caught her and pulled her back against him. For a moment, his lips were against the nape of her neck, warm and tender.

"Don't, don't!" she whispered.

He let her go at last with a reluctant sigh. She kept her back to him.

"I told you once, there would be a time for us, Corliss. I haven't forgotten it. I haven't given up on it. There will be a time."

She pulled open the door and stepped quickly inside. The latch clicked behind her. With fumbling fingers, she hurried to turn the key and fasten the chain, as if to lock him out of her life forever. In a moment, she heard steps going down he hall. He had gone.

Then, making up her mind swiftly, she reached for the phone and checked the flights home. If she hurried, she could catch one yet tonight. She had scarcely unpacked anything. She hastily gathered her things, left a message for Dr. Williams in case he tried to reach her, paid her hotel bill, and caught a cab.

It wasn't until she was airborne a couple of hours later that she began to feel safe. Reese would not come to her room again, could not phone her. He could not lure her into seeing him again.

Oh, why had she ever let him into her room? Why had she listened to what he'd said about poor Jennie, about his unhappiness?

The flight home took a scant hour and a half. Soon, she was getting her car out of the parking lot and driving away. Father was not expecting her until tomorrow. If she arrived early, he would wonder why. How could she tell him? She turned in the direction of Elizabeth's apartment.

A card game was in session at Sadie's Place. It was a particularly tense one. Cassiday had been winning again, and Tom Whittier was his victim. Tom wiped his brow, loosened his tie, and kept a stiff grin on his face. But he wasn't bluffing anyone and he knew it.

"One more hand," Tom said. "Then that's it for tonight."

Cassiday dealt the cards. A slender cigar was clenched between his teeth. A

278

crowd had gathered. The pot was a big one. Tom was down to his last bet. His pay envelope had gone dry. He had signed paper in the amount of six hundred dollars.

"Let's see what you've got," Cassiday said.

He said a prayer, was afraid to look. A murmur went up through the crowd. He had a good hand. But with that cold smile he had grown to loathe, Cassiday flipped over his cards.

"You lose, mister."

The sickening feeling in Tom's stomach was stronger than ever. He watched Cassiday rake in all the money – his money and his I.O.U. – and got shakily to his feet. He needed air.

He stumbled away from the table and crossed the outer room to the screen door. He thought he was going to be sick. Then he walked across the porch, down the steps, and away toward town. He'd sold his car because of Cassiday, so now he was on foot.

It was a long, hot walk back to his

apartment. He didn't have cab fare, not even bus fare. How could he have gone back a second time when he'd lost so heavily before? How could he have let Cassiday get his hooks in him again?

Reaching his apartment, Tom went in without turning on a light. He flung himself across the bed. It took a moment for him to realize he was not alone. He sat up with a start and reached out to turn on a lamp.

"Leave it off," a harsh voice said.

"What is this? Who are you? How did you get in here?"

"Doesn't matter. How would you like to make a couple of thousand, Tom?"

"What?"

"A couple of thousand."

"What is this? A joke?"

"No joke. It's on the level."

"Who is it? Your voice is familiar –"

"Never mind about that now. Do you want a couple of thousand?"

"You know I need it! You set me up, didn't you, with Cassiday?"

The laugh was low, ugly. "Listen,

you're in a bind, Tom. All you have to do is come in with us."

"What have I got to do?"

"Build something for us. Being an engineer, I figure you can handle it. That's why I picked you."

Tom held his thumping head. "What do I build?"

"Lab equipment."

Tom got to his feet. The Gilman project, of course.

"I see you know what I'm talking about, Tom."

"What is it you want me to do?"

"Build Unit One."

"Gilman's Unit? But how?"

Cigar smoke came wafting toward him. "We'll show you how, Tom."

"One unit won't do you any good! It takes both units—"

"So, we steal the one you're building at Mitchell's place. We'll have them both . . . Think about it, Tom. You're over a barrel. There's money in it for you. You need it."

"And if I don't go along with you?"

"I wouldn't want to think about that, Tom. Cassiday can get mean. You've got no idea."

Tom licked his lips. His hands were shaking. "I guess I don't have any choice."

"Now you're talking," the voice said.

XXI

Burr Kaldner was in a foul mood. Nothing was going right. They'd lost the Wagner contract to Mitchell Electronics. Drew Fielding was learning fast. Maybe too fast. Then there was Jennie. His dearest Jennie. She seemed frailer to him every day. He had insisted that she and Reese stay in the house with him. "It's big enough for us all. I won't crowd you or intrude on your privacy. Stay, enjoy it. Besides, it's Jennie's home."

Reese Sheridan had listened to that, saying nothing. But he had agreed and not too reluctantly. In fact, Burr suspected the man was relieved, even pleased with the idea.

It was late when Burr left his office. He was worried about Jennie. Reese had gone to Chicago to make a contact or two with some important people. Burr lighted a cigar and twisted it in his fingers, wondering if that had been a good move. He knew the boy had charm. Good looks. A presence. Something he didn't have himself. That was one of the reasons he had wanted Reese in his organization. The other being that he wanted to rub John Mitchell the wrong way. He smiled thinking about that. In this business, a man had to watch all the angles, grab the brass ring and ride with it.

Burr got into his big car, started the engine with a roar, and drove away, turning on the air conditioning against the heat of the day. He thought of Sadie's Place and wanted to go there. But Jennie was home alone, except for the nurse he'd hired, and he felt he must not tarry along the way.

The drive home took but a few minutes. He found Jennie waiting for him. The sight of her in the wheelchair tore at his heart. "Hello, honey," he said.

He bent and kissed her cheek.

She laughed and gave him a hug. "You're late."

"Business. A desk full of work."

"That's because Reese is away, isn't it? Things have piled up without his help."

His daughter seemed so pathetically eager for Reese to be important in the office, for his presence to be felt.

"Of course. But he'll be home soon."

Jennie laughed and held to his hand. "I can hardly wait."

He tried to hide a frown. Reese Sheridan wasn't exactly the man he would have chosen for Jennie. But that didn't matter. Jennie had wanted him, and now she had him.

"Do you feel like going out for a ride tonight?" he asked.

"Oh, maybe. We'll see."

"Are you all right?" he asked, unable to keep the alarm out of his voice. "Your cold hasn't come back? I thought you were over it."

"Oh, Daddy! I wish you wouldn't be like that," Jennie replied quickly. "Of course I'm all right. You always fret so. Like an old mother hen."

He laughed. "So, I do. Because you're my own little girl, and I love you."

A frown crossed Jennie's face. "You'd do anything for me, wouldn't you?"

"Almost."

"Would you buy me a husband?"

Burr felt the swift kick of surprise against his ribs. "What do you mean?"

"Why did Reese marry me – all of a sudden?"

Burr clenched the cigar in his teeth. "He loves you."

"Does he really, Daddy, or did he marry me because he felt sorry for me? Or because you offered to make him vice-president?"

Burr gripped her hands in his. His heart was thudding. He was consumed with the need to protect her, to tell her whatever she wanted to hear. "Honey, I made him vice-president because he deserved it, be-cause I needed a good right-hand man! I know my business. If there's one thing I know – it's that!"

"Daddy, you know about business. But –"

"If I thought Reese didn't love you, I'd – I'd –" He swallowed hard and reached out to touch her pale cheek. "Has he mistreated you? Is he making you unhappy?"

Tears came to Jennie's eyes. "Oh, no! Not that, Daddy. He's so good. So kind. So sweet. It's not that—"

"Then, what? For God's sake, what?" he demanded.

"He felt sorry for me, didn't he? Because of the accident. Because he thinks he was to blame."

"Maybe," Burr nodded. "But a man doesn't marry someone because of something like that! He took the accident hard. I think that's when he realized how much you meant to him." Jennie wanted so very badly to believe. He could see it in her eyes. He smiled at her. "Don't question, pet. Don't doubt. Reese will be home in a couple of days and everything will be all right again. You miss him, don't you?"

"I die of loneliness when he's away," she whispered. "Oh, Daddy, I love him so much—"

"Of course you do. And you're happy with him, aren't you?"

"Yes. Yes!"

"Well, let's have dinner," Burr said. "Then we're going for a drive. Where would you like to go?"

"Out to the country. Past that big house with the horses in the meadow."

Burr nodded and felt sick to his stomach. She'd always wanted a horse of her own, and he would never permit it. Now it was too late.

They ate dinner at the large dining room table, and Burr ate wolfishly, just as he always did when he was angry or upset, which seemed to be most of the time.

Two hours later they went outside, and he lifted Jennie into the car, shocked to find how tiny and delicate she was. In a rush of hate, he wanted to throttle Reese Sheridan. Reese had been driving that night. No matter what had happened on the highway, Reese had been driving! He was responsible.

They drove away from Seabourne and out to the house that Jennie wanted to see. For nearly an hour, until the dark caught them, she watched the horses in the meadow, running, feeding, nuzzling colts.

A bit of color came to her face. She laughed. His heart swelled.

At last they drove home. He carried Jennie up to her room for the nurse to put her to bed. He said goodnight and left her. He went downstairs to his elaborate den and looked at his watch. A call he was expecting was due. Eleven o'clock. No later. What was holding things up?

He stomped around the room, fists knotted. His nerves were on edge. If this deal came off, it would deflate John Mitchell as he had never been deflated before. Burr laughed coarsely at the idea.

The phone rang. He answered it.

"Everything's set," the voice said.

"You're positive? You've got this wrapped up tight?"

"Positive. Rest easy, Burr. Everything's under control, just like I planned."

"It had better be," Burr snapped.

There was a pause on the other end of the line. Burr had made his point. He slammed up the receiver. It had to work. He couldn't remember when he'd wanted anything more than this. It would put a crimp in John Mitchell and Drew Fielding that wouldn't be easily ironed out. He laughed aloud. Then he treated himself to a new cigar and sat with his feet up on the desk, contemplating the whole deal. Deals popped up in the funniest places. Men thirsty for money were everywhere. He understood them. They talked his language. He hadn't got where he was today by wearing white gloves. So what if a little dirt had rubbed off on him? No one was truly clean these days. Everybody had his price.

The next morning when Burr left the house, Jennie was still sleeping. She seemed a little tired these days, and it worried him. At the office, he used a private entrance, in no mood for his secretary or any of his work force. It was ten o'clock before he unlocked his door, called in his accountant, and began handling the mountain of paper work that waited for him. It was past eleven when he glanced up and saw Reese going toward his office. What was he doing home today? He wasn't due until tomorrow!

"Reese?"

Reese paused.

"Come in here!" Burr called. He sent the accountant scurrying away, and in a moment, Reese was in the doorway – briefcase in his hand. "Sit down. Shut the door."

Reese took the chair in front of his desk, crossed his legs, and waited.

"Why are you home early?"

Reese lighted a cigarette and smiled coolly. "Work was finished. Why not come home? Besides, I was anxious about Jennie."

"How did it go in Chicago?"

Reese snapped open his briefcase and tossed the contracts across to him. "Signed, sealed, delivered."

"Our terms?"

"Better than our terms."

Burr lifted his brows. "You're learning, Reese."

"I sure am," he murmured.

"What did you say? Speak up! You know I hate for people to mumble. If you've got something to say, say it!''

Reese eyed him with his green eyes, not moving a muscle, just watching him. "If that's all, I'll get back to my own office," Reese said.

"Sit down! I never told you to go," Burr said. "I want to talk to you."

Burr watched Reese lower his long frame to the chair again. Reese hated his gall. Sometimes it was apparent by the look on his face. It was on the tip of his tongue to tell Reese about the new deal. Then he changed his mind. Reese wouldn't like it. Reese was still too easy, too afraid to put his nose in where it wasn't wanted. Well, the boy would learn – one way or another – that sometimes, that was all a man could do if he wanted to get ahead.

"I want to talk to you about Jennie," Burr said.

Reese eyed him with his green eyes, not moving a muscle.

"Didn't you phone her last night?" Burr asked.

"Of course!"

"Was she sick?"

292

"No! She said you'd gone for a drive in the country. She sounded very cheerful –"

"Good."

"What is it?" Reese asked.

Burr looked at his son-in-law and got slowly to his feet. "She thinks you feel sorry for her."

"Anyone would," Reese shot back.

"She thinks you married her because you feel guilty about the accident."

Reese was on his feet now too. "What did you tell her?"

Burr puffed on his cigar. Reese came striding across the room to him. "What did you tell her, Burr?" he asked anxiously.

"That you loved her. That the accident made you realize it."

Reese sagged. His face went to a tired look. He nodded. "Good."

"Why is she doubting you, all of a sudden?" Burr demanded.

Reese stared at him. "I have no idea."

"You're not making her happy."

"I am!" Reese said and bitterness

swept over him. "I am. I do everything I can! What more can you ask of me?"

Burr shifted the cigar in his mouth. "She senses something."

"She's wrong!"

"Maybe."

Reese moved to the door and the anger was deep in his green eyes. "What do you want of me, Burr? What more can I give than I'm already giving?"

"You make her happy," Burr said evenly. "You erase every doubt she's got or you're going to be the sorriest man alive!"

"You like playing God, don't you?"

Burr laughed shortly, coldly. "You're on the receiving end, remember? You got what you wanted, didn't you?"

Reese stalked out of the room, slamming the door behind him. Burr tapped the ash from his cigar into a huge ashtray and smiled to himself. He expected he would see a change in Jennie shortly. Any day now. Reese was no fool. He'd toe the line as long as he kept the whip close to his back, just a fraction of an inch away from striking him.

Reese, when all was said, knew how to play his cards.

XXII

Work had begun on Roberts Mill. Strange cars were in the woods – trucks, construction men. Sounds of hammering and sawing filled the days, and while Corliss did not go there herself, she heard about it through Drew.

Drew, as had become his habit, came nearly every evening to see her father. He would come striding through the woods, Fuzz at his heels, smoking his pipe, a large brown envelope under his arm.

Then, in the cool twilight, on the patio, he would talk about the office and the problems there. Drew was managing very well. So well in fact, that her father was thinking of never going back, even though he was physically able now to spend at least a few hours a day behind his desk.

"What about Burr?" Father asked.

Drew frowned. "All's very quiet with

him. It worries me."

"He's a man to watch anytime, but when he drops out of sight, something's brewing."

Corliss leaned back in the lawn chair, studying the sky. The sun set so early these evenings. But the twilights were especially delightful.

"Paul's angry with me," Drew said. "Over Unit Two. I've been riding Tom Whittier as hard as I can. I don't know which way to jump!"

"Paul will wait," Father said confidently. "He has to. It would be foolish for him to drop us after we've already done so much. If he switches horses in the middle of the stream, think what it would cost him in time and money."

"The entire project is very important, John. I've made a few inquiries. If Paul gets a patent and we put the equipment on the market, it could make Paul a rich man. And the manufacturer who builds it will make a buck, too. We can't afford to lose it, John."

"What about Tom?" John asked.

"What's the delay?"

"I don't honestly know. I keep getting the feeling he's stalling. But why? I only know he's stopped going to Sadie's Place. Still, he disappears immediately after work as if the very devil were after him. No one knows where he goes or what he does."

"Love affair?" Corliss asked.

"Tom? I don't think so. I suppose it's possible."

They fell silent then, each lost in their own thoughts. Then Madeline Huffman was mentioned and the work being done at the mill.

"Have you seen it, Corliss?" Drew asked.

"No!" she said with a shake of her head.

"Nor have I. I think I'll walk down that way. Why don't you come along?"

"Father can go with you," Corliss said quickly.

"Too far for me," Father said. "Run along, Corliss. Keep Drew company."

She didn't want to go. Father was

looking steadily at her, and Drew was waiting. They both knew the old mill was all mixed up in her heart with Reese. Why did they want to do this to her?

"Sometimes, you have to bite on the nail," Drew said quietly. "Besides, you need some fresh air, and the walk will do you good. You've been keeping yourself cooped up at the lab far too much.

She relented and decided to go. There had to be a first time she supposed, and it might be easier to see it with someone than to go alone.

The path was cool, shadowy, and the night dew would soon fall. Fuzz trotted ahead of them, happy, and it was pleasant in the woods this time of day.

They reached the mill a few minutes later. From the distance it looked the same, and Corliss caught her breath. Oh, it was lovely here! Such a dear, memorable place. Tears stung her eyes.

"Let's go inside," Drew said.

She was reluctant to step through the door. But once she did, she found that it didn't bother her. There was scaffolding, the smell of new wood, evidence of repairs being made against the damage the weather had done. It was the same and yet different.

"It's coming along very well," Drew said, surprised.

"Yes."

"Madeline told me it was, but I didn't quite believe they could progress so fast."

"Madeline Huffman. The mystery woman."

"She's done the community a service," Drew replied. "No one else had thought to do this."

"Why? Why is she doing it?" Corliss wondered.

"She likes to be busy."

"Couldn't she have been busy elsewhere?"

Drew gave her a quick look. "I suppose so."

"But she came here. I've wondered about that."

"Have you?"

"You knew her before, didn't you?"

Drew struck a match and held it above

his pipe. His gray eyes were shadowy, and he did not look at her again.

"Let's see what they've done to the wheel," he said.

"Drew, I want to know!"

He ignored her. He began walking away, and Corliss in a sudden, childish manner, stamped her foot. "Drew, I want to know about you and Madeline Huffman!"

He turned back. "If you don't come along, brat, I'm going to leave you here to all the spooks."

She followed him quickly enough. The subject of Madeline didn't come up again. They walked almost silently, and when they reached her house, she said a curt goodnight and went inside. Drew whistled for Fuzz, and in a moment he had gone, disappearing into the darkness.

The next morning at the lab, Elizabeth seemed very quiet.

"Problems?" Corliss asked.

Elizabeth nodded. "I heard from Alex last night. He wants to see me. He's in town for a week."

"Elizabeth, do I detect hesitation in your voice?"

Elizabeth gave her a smile. "Yes, it's going to be goodbye this time. Everything's so uncertain with Alex. I've given it a lot of thought and Alex isn't for me."

"I hear you talking, Elizabeth. But the minute Alex smiles at you – something happens to your good sense."

"Not this time. Paul asked me out on the weekend. I accepted."

Corliss blinked with surprise. "I don't understand. Alex tonight. Paul on the weekend. This isn't like you!"

"I like Paul, a lot, Corliss. But I want to be sure I'm really over Alex. That I can put him in the past, where he belongs."

"I wish you luck, old dear."

Corliss thought of Reese. He belonged in the past too. But had she succeeded in putting him there?

Corliss went to open the large envelope that had come in the morning mail. Many of their tests came to them this way. Or by messenger. She opened the envelope and poured out onto the desk all the little sealed bottles and the boxed slides. She began sorting through them. She and Elizabeth usually divided the work.

"What's this!" she said in surprise. Her hand trembled as she picked up the slide and read the name on the box. "It's Jennie!"

"What's wrong?" Elizabeth asked. "What's wrong with Jennie?"

"I'll tell you in a minute."

Corliss took the slide to her lab bench, put it under the microscope and looked at it. She didn't want to trust her eyes or believe what she saw.

"Elizabeth, check this, will you? Please?"

Elizabeth was only a few moments. Then she looked up, and nodded her head.

"You were right, Corliss. Jennie has virus pneumonia!"

XXIII

Drew reached his office early that day. He was determined to have it out with Tom Whittier. But Tom was late coming in, and the first thing Drew knew, he was involved in other things. When his secretary put through a personal call, he expected it to be John Mitchell, or perhaps Corliss. He should have known it would be neither.

"I'll make it brief, Drew," Madeline Huffman said. "I want to see you. Tonight. It's important."

"It's always important with you, isn't it?"

"Don't be bitter, Drew. Please. I'm not kidding. This is important."

"All right. I'll stop by on my way home. Will that do?"

"Bless you, Drew. You just made my day."

Drew hung up and wondered what she wanted now. Most of the time she lured him there on one pretext or another about Roberts Mill. Some legal matter that he could have answered over the phone. Or she simply wanted to talk to him because she was lonely.

It had to end. Now. Before it went any further. Why hadn't he done it before? Perhaps because by nature he was not a person who liked to tread heavily on anyone. Was that why he'd let this thing with Tom Whittier drag on and on? If John had been here, it would never have happened.

Tom was unavailable when he phoned his office again.

"He's out in the machine shop, Mr. Fielding," Drew was told. "I'll leave a message you phoned."

It was about ten o'clock when Paul Gilman arrived. Paul was not a big man. He always had the look of the indoors about him. Behind his glasses, his brown eyes were sleepy, almost dull. But he knew that the eyes were hiding a very alert and intelligent brain.

"Hello, Paul."

"You know why I'm here," Paul said.

Drew nodded. "I do. And I can't blame you. I have been trying to get in touch with Tom all morning, but we keep missing connections. Would you like to go out to the plant and see what progress he's made?"

"I know what progress he's made," Paul said pointedly. "It's not enough."

Drew spread his hands out on the top of his desk. How could he stall this impatient man one more time? How?

"If I don't see something constructive within the next three days, Drew, I'm pulling out."

Drew felt the sting of shock. John thought this wouldn't happen. "Might I ask if—"

"Burr Kaldner? For your information, yes. Burr's interested. Very interested. He'll absorb any loss that I must take here. I'm sorry, Drew. I don't like pressuring anyone. Three days. Friday night. Five o'clock."

Drew nodded. "That seems fair enough, Paul."

Paul got to his feet He stretched out a hand, and Drew shook it. Then Paul was gone, slipping away quietly, a stooped, worried man.

Drew knew about the time someone had been in Paul's office. He knew about the tracings. Corliss had told him in confidence. Could Tom be involved some way? He punched the button on his phone. "Get Tom Whittier. I don't care where he is or what he's doing. Tell him to be in my office within five minutes!"

He slammed the receiver, anger burning him. Not only because he was angry with Tom, but because he was angry with himself. The last thing in the world he wanted to do was let Burr Kaldner take over Paul's project. He was convinced the two units were worth their weight in gold.

Tom arrived ten minutes later, tie loosened, shirt collar unbuttoned. He looked tired. Dark circles were under his eyes, and his hands were trembling as he toyed with a pencil. He sat before Drew's desk like a man sentenced to death.

"You know what I want, Tom?"

"Sure."

"I'll tell you how it is. Paul has given us until Friday. Then the whole project is going to Burr Kaldner."

Tom licked his lips. "I'm getting close to finishing it. There have been all kinds of headaches. Paul's plans looked right on paper, but they didn't prove out. I've put it to all sorts of tests. I wanted to be sure—"

"I appreciate your efforts along those lines. I want to know if I can plan on a finished unit by Friday evening at five o'clock."

Tom nodded slowly. "Yes. I'll have it ready."

"All right. That's all I wanted to hear."

"What about Unit One?" Tom asked. "Will Paul present it then? Will we make a trial run of the two units together?"

"I didn't ask him. He ordered Unit Two. We promised to deliver. Beyond that —we're not obligated—"

"All right. I'll get busy on it, Drew. I'll

finish it."

Drew got to his feet. He leaned his palms on the top of the desk and gave Tom Whittier a direct look. "We'll put it this way, Tom. If you don't deliver – you'll be given your severance pay."

Tom swallowed hard. "But, Mr. Fielding, I –" He muttered something to himself. Then he turned and walked out the door. Drew sighed. He'd hated doing that. But what else could he do? He'd already gone out on the limb for Tom countless times.

Drew spent a busy day at his desk. At lunchtime, he had his secretary send out for coffee and sandwiches. He didn't leave the plant until after five thirty. Then, with a tired sigh, he remembered that he'd promised to stop by Madeline's.

The drive out of the city took longer than usual. The skies had grown cloudy, and another summer storm seemed in the making. Madeline's house looked snug and comfortable in the growing twilight. The air was turning cooler. He smelled autumn in the air.

Madeline waited for him in her doorway. She was delectable. So cool and poised. Her voice flowed over him like a warm mist, easing the tension and the headache that kept trying to surface.

"Hello, Madeline."

"I took the liberty of fixing us an early dinner."

"But Mrs. Petrie will be expecting me."

Madeline smiled and shook her head. "No. I phoned her. She seemed rather glad not to have to prepare dinner. I got the impression she had some errands to take care of." Madeline linked her arm through his. The house had a comfortable air about it. "Sit here, darling. I've fixed you a cocktail."

"I'm not a drinking man."

"I remember. But this is something special. Very light and relaxing. My own recipe."

"Then I should beware," he said.

She laughed. Soon, he found himself on the comfortable divan, feet up, jacket off, the cool, tinkling glass pressed into his hand. There was music. Low. Muted. His headache began to leave. Madeline was lighting candles on the table on the patio, fussing with things in the kitching, managing to look sophisticated and elegant in a lacy apron.

"If you're ready, the food is," she said at last.

He wasn't hungry. But the meal proved to be tasty and tempting. He ate more than he should. Perhaps because if he ate, he wouldn't have to talk. And talking to Madeline tonight seemed filled with hidden dangers. She could take anything he said and twist it around until she was talking about the past and what they had meant to each other then.

At last, over a final cup of coffee, the dishes cleared away, Drew lighted his pipe and braced himself for her finale.

But she fooled him. She was not an easy woman to reckon with, and now, when he had expected her to deal her ace card, she abruptly changed the subject to the old mill.

"Construction is coming along so well.

By the last of the month or the first of October, we should be all done. Open to the public. Can't you imagine how it will look? The autumn color of the woods, the huge old wheel turning again, spilling water? We've agreed there should be a small souvenir shop where we can sell photographs and booklets."

"You've been busy."

"Ah, yes. But Corliss Mitchell has been a disappointment."

Drew set his jaw. "She didn't really want to be on your committee, you know."

"But she loves the old mill! I know she does."

"Yes."

"Then why—"

Drew got to his feet. He stood looking out to the woods, across the green of Madeline's lawn, and knew perfectly well why Corliss no longer was enchanted with the mill. It brought back painful memories of Reese Sheridan, a man she had loved and lost, but still loved.

Madeline came to stand beside him.

312

She linked her arm through his and leaned her head against his sleeve.

"It's so lovely here this time of day. I thought I saw a deer early this morning."

"It's possible. There are a few around. I've put out some salt licks. In the winter, I usually try to feed them when the snow's on."

"How like you!" She tightened her fingers around his arm. "Drew, I want to be serious for a moment."

Now it was coming? "About what?"

"Us."

"There is no 'us.' I thought you understood that."

"I love you, Drew. I never stopped loving you."

He smiled at that. "Oh, but you did. When it was convenient for you to do so."

Her hand dropped away. "You're being mean."

"No. Just truthful."

"Can you doubt I love you?"

"Perhaps not. But it's one-sided, Madeline."

He saw the hurt in her eyes. It hurt him

in turn. "I'm sorry," he said.

Madeline lifted her chin. "Who is she?"

"What?"

"Who is she?"

"No one."

Madeline scoffed. "I don't believe you. Not for a minute, Drew Fielding. If there wasn't someone, you'd come back to me. I know you would."

Drew fished in his pocket for his pipe and slowly filled it with tobacco. He lighted a match and held it above the bowl. She was staring at him, two red spots of color in her cheeks.

"It's Corliss, isn't it? You've been in love with her all along."

"Madeline!"

"Oh, don't pretend with me. I've seen you with her. I've seen how it is!"

"Corliss is like a sister. I've always looked after her! Don't be ridiculous."

"I'm not. But if you're denying it, then you're the ridiculous one. Now, if you don't mind, I'd like for you to leave. Before you see me cry—"

She rushed away from him. He stood there for a moment, stunned. Then he gathered his coat and moved to the door.

"Drew—"

"Yes, Madeline."

"I'm sorry. I must have sounded like some jealous schoolgirl."

He smiled at that. "I'm sorry too, Madeline. Find someone else. Be happy. I'd like that."

"Are you saying goodbye?"

"Yes. Think back, Madeline. I never really said hello. It was you that did that."

She blinked fast. He had to admire her in that moment. But it was like her. She could face up to things when she had to. Just as she had when she'd met her late husband. She had faced up to fundamental truths, and when she had, she'd been quick enough to say goodbye, to leave him standing there with a bleeding heart. Now, it had come full circle, and he found he must do the same to her. He didn't find it pleasant. He didn't enjoy it.

"What am I to do?" she asked.

"Go home," he said gently. "Or if you

stay – find someone else."

"I've made a terrible mess of it, haven't I?"

"No. I have. I shouldn't have let it start. Goodnight. Madeline."

He walked out of the house and got inside his car. He wouldn't come here again, no matter what. Not until she clearly understood it was over before it had begun, that when they had parted years ago, it had been for good. But what had she meant about Corliss? Did she really think he was in love with her? He paused for a moment before starting the motor. Corliss! He smiled. The name evoked so many pictures in his mind's eye. Corliss chasing Fuzz, windblown and suntanned, laughing, teasing him, or suddenly appearing in his den, coming in as if it were her own home, making herself comfortable.

Corliss!

He started the motor. He drove slowly, in no hurry to get home. He hadn't gone far when he heard a peculiar thumping sound and knew that he had a flat tire. It was dark. He discovered he had no flashlight. He'd leave the car, walk home and come back for it in the morning. Jacket slung over his shoulder, he walked along slowly, enjoying the night, following the familiar road, whistling softly. Corliss! Now and then the name came to the surface of his heart and lingered there like a warm flame. He didn't let this happen often. It hadn't been wise. But now that Madeline had brought it out in the open, he found he couldn't tuck it away in some convenient corner of his mind. Corliss was there, wherever he looked, wherever he turned. She was there, all the long, lovely length of her, all soft hair and quiet eyes, all sweetness and warmth.

He reached the house and found it dark. Mrs. Petrie had already retired or had perhaps gone out. He went to the kitchen and got a glass of milk and carried it back to the den.

He played with the thought of phoning Corliss, just to hear her voice, and quickly decided against it. At such a vulnerable moment, he might blurt out something he shouldn't. He wished it would rain, thunder, lightning, lash out with sweeping winds. It would clear the air. Perhaps it would clear his mind as well. But would it clear his heart of Corliss?

He might as well admit it. Let it out into the open. How could he hide it from himself any longer? No. He would never be clear of Corliss Mitchell. Never in a million years. He had loved her far too long for that!

318

XXIV

Jennie had caught the flu. It had been a severe attack, and since she wasn't strong, there had been complications. Now, worst of all, pneumonia had set in. Burr would not allow them to take her to the hospital. She had begged to stay at home. Burr hired two additional nurses so that there was someone with her around the clock, and had a doctor on constant call.

The large house became as quiet as a tomb. Burr would not have Jennie disturbed in any way. He spent long hours beside her bed, talking with her when she was able, stroking her hand, watching her sleep, praying that she would be well soon.

Reese had been faithful. Burr had to say that much for him. Reese went to work every day at Jennie's insistence, but when he came home, it was the highlight

319

of her day.

Upon rising, Burr dressed quickly and made straight for Jennie's room, praying each day to see some improvement.

The September sun was warm in the room. There were flowers and a mountain of greeting cards. Jennie was awake. She gave him a wan smile.

"Hello, Daddy."

"How's my sweetheart? Feeling better?"

"Much better," Jennie murmured.

He wanted to believe it. But his eyes told him it wasn't true, and when he glanced at the nurse hovering nearby, he saw the expression of compassion in her eyes. His heart thudded heavily in his chest, and it was difficult for him to breathe.

"You're going to be up in no time at all," he said, squeezing Jennie's hand.

"Of course," Jennie said tiredly. "Where's Reese?"

"Didn't he stop in?"

"Yes. But I want to see him again."

"I think he's downstairs. I'll call him."

He tiptoed out of the room. Then he hurried down the wide, carpeted stairs to the dining room where Reese was hidden behind the morning paper. With an angry motion, Burr ripped it out of his hands. "Why do you dally here when Jennie wants you?"

Anger flashed across Reese's handsome face. "I've seen Jennie. I'll see her again before I leave for the office. I'd like my breakfast in peace, Burr."

Burr knotted his fists. He wanted to lose his temper as he used to in the old days. Lately, he found it necessary more and more to keep it under control.

Reese softened. He put the paper aside. "Burr, perhaps Jennie should go to the hospital, for her own good."

"No! She wants to stay here. She'll stay. I'll bring in anything she needs. Any equipment – anything!"

Reese nodded. "Well, I suppose it might be best in the long run. I'll go up now."

Reese strode away, and in a moment, Burr followed and hovered outside the door. It had been left ajar, but Reese and Jennie were alone. The nurse had stepped out. Burr saw Reese bend over Jennie and kiss her lightly.

"You look even better than you did half an hour ago," Reese said.

Jennie laughed. "You're getting to be a better liar every day."

"Nonsense! There's even a hint of color in your face."

"Temperature."

"No," Reese said. "The blush of roses. I'll bring you some tonight. What color? Red, white, yellow—"

Jennie reached up and pulled Reese down to her again. Burr clamped a cigar between his lips as he watched from the hall.

"Say you love me," Jennie sighed. "Please, Reese, say you love me!"

"You know I do."

"Say it as if you really mean it. Just once I'd like to hear you say it like that."

Burr wanted to rush in and take Reese Sheridan by the nape of his neck and shake him until the words came out as

Jennie wanted them.

Reese bent low again and whispered to Jennie. Then Jennie was clinging to him, her eyes glowing. Burr turned away, taking a handkerchief out of his pocket, blowing his nose.

"Phone call, Mr. Kaldner," the nurse said.

"I'll take it here in the hall," he said. "I'm expecting it." He snatched up the receiver. "What's the report?"

"Everything's going to work out. I've about got the final plans made."

"Just a minute." Reese was coming out of Jennie's room, and Burr covered the mouthpiece with his big hand. "How does she seem to you?"

"Fair," Reese murmured. "Perhaps a little more fatigued. I'm going now."

He waited until Reese had disappeared down the steps, then he turned back to the phone. He talked for several minutes, his voice rising at times with fervor and anger, receding again as he listened. "There can be no foul-up. Understand? I've got my neck out on this. Way out!"

There was a laugh on the other end of the line and then the slam of the receiver. The man was getting pretty cocky about it all. He thought he was going to pull it off, but there was many a slip between the cup and the lip.

"Daddy –" He heard Jennie calling. He hurried back into her room. "What is it, pet?"

"What was the phone call?"

"Business."

"What kind of business?"

He shook his head. "I won't bother your head with it. Just let your Daddy handle it."

"Do me a favor?"

"Anything! All you have to do is ask, honey."

"I want to talk to Corliss Mitchell. Will you have her come to see me? Right away –"

Burr got to his feet. "Why would you want to see her?"

"I must see her, that's all."

Burr tried to protest, and Jennie shook her head.

"Please, don't argue. Just bring her!"

"All right. I'll bring her, Jennie. You try to rest now."

He left the room. He would go straight to the Gilman Laboratories and find Corliss Mitchell. He would bring her here. Whatever Jennie wanted, she was going to get! His poor little girl. So sick. So frail.

He drove his big car through the morning traffic and straight to the laboratory. Without hesitation, he went up the steps and inside. Through a glass door, he caught sight of Corliss bent over her microscope. He knocked at the door with his big fist, and she looked up. Without waiting, he pushed open the door.

"What can we do for you, Mr. Kaldner?" Elizabeth Lane asked.

"I want Corliss."

Corliss thrust her hands into the pockets of her lab coat. "I don't understand."

"It's Jennie. She's asked to see you." He took three steps into the room and was prepared to snatch the girl by the arm and force her away if necessary. "She's very ill. She asked me to bring you. Come.''

"Now?''

"Now!''

Corliss looked at Burr with steady eyes and after a moment, took off her white lab coat, picked up her purse, and walked out of the room ahead of him. He tried to tell her about Jennie as they drove through the city to the house.

"I'm aware of her condition, Mr. Kaldner. I've run every test the doctor has sent to the lab.''

"Oh.''

She would say no more. She sat very quietly beside him, hands in her lap, staring out the window. She looked a little pale and tense. A few minutes later, they had entered the house, and Burr led the way up the stairs to Jennie's room.

"In here,'' he said.

Jennie was awake. She saw Corliss, and for a moment the two women stared at each other.

"Hello, Jennie,'' Corliss said.

"Leave us, Daddy,'' Jennie said.

Burr could do nothing but turn away

and step out to the hall. There, he paced up and down. He could hear the murmur of their voices, but couldn't distinguish words. It seemed Corliss was in there for an hour. In reality, it was more like fifteen minutes. Then she came to the door and stood there for a moment. There was compassion in her eyes.

"Will you call me a cab, Mr. Kaldner? I'm ready to go back to the lab now," Corliss said.

"I'll drive you."

"Thank you. I prefer a cab."

He stared at her, and he saw the steel beneath the soft curves of her tall body, the metal sparking in her eyes. Burr reached for the phone, called a cab, and told her it would be there shortly.

"Thank you. I'll wait outside for it."

"Miss Mitchell —"

"Yes?" she paused at the top of the stairs, hand on the railing.

Burr swallowed hard. "What did Jennie want with you? What in God's name did she want with you?"

Corliss gave him a short smile. "That's

none of your business, Mr. Kaldner.''

Then she was gone. Well, Jennie would tell him. Jennie told him everything. But when he went back into her room, Jennie refused to discuss it. The nurse asked him to leave. He was left to wonder, and it wasn't a comfortable role for him. He had always been in command of everything but this time – he swore to himself. Corliss Mitchell! Jennie still doubted her husband. It was that simple. He'd have another talk with that boy. He'd twist his arm a little harder. Reese would come around. He'd make Jennie know she was loved, truly loved. Reese would do whatever he was told to do. Or else –

In the cab, Corliss huddled in one corner, her heart thudding painfully. She hoped she never had to endure another day like this.

The moment the door had closed behind her in Jennie's room, Jennie had motioned for her to step up closer to the bed.

''I won't keep you long, Corliss,''

Jennie had said. "I promise."

"How are you?"

"That doesn't matter. Only one thing matters."

"Why have you sent for me, Jennie?" Corliss asked.

"Because of Reese. You still love him, don't you, Corliss?"

"Jennie, please —"

"I took him away from you. But I love him too, Corliss. I love him so much! I've loved him for so long —"

"— he feels responsible, you know," Jennie went on. "Because of the accident. That's why he married me. I know that's why —"

Corliss closed her eyes for a moment. The girl wanted so desperately to be told it wasn't true. Somehow, Corliss found her voice. "Reese loves you, Jennie. I know. Perhaps he does feel responsible for the accident, but that doesn't change the fact that he loves you."

Jennie's big blue eyes were suddenly very wide, very searching. "How?" she asked in a desperate voice. "How do you know?'' Her thin hand gripped Corliss's tightly.

''Because he told me, Jennie. When he came to tell me he was going to marry you. He told me then.''

''And you believed him?''

''How could I believe anything else?''

''But the accident –''

''Sometimes, Jennie, it takes things like that to wake us up.''

For a moment, a stifling silence was in the room. Jennie lay very still. Then a new look came to her face. ''Corliss –''

''Yes?''

''When I'm gone, tell him for me, that I never blamed him for the accident. Not for a minute did I blame him.''

''You mustn't talk like this, Jennie. You're going to be well again! Soon.''

Jennie's smile was faint, a wisp of a thing soon gone. ''Tell him.''

''Jennie –''

''He's made me happy. At your expense. I know – how much you loved him. I – I came between you. Can you forgive me?''

Corliss had never felt so compassionate for anyone in her life. Never had she been so touched. Jennie appealed to every gentle, decent fiber of her being. Somehow she had to help the girl, set her mind at ease.

"We change, Jennie. We think we love someone and find that we don't," Corliss said.

"You don't love Reese anymore?" she asked surprised. "Is that what you're saying?"

"Yes."

"But how, I mean—"

"How can I be so sure? It's simple. When you fall in love with someone else — how can you still love another man?"

Jennie tried to raise up in bed, her eyes luminous. "You love someone else? But who?"

Corliss was caught in her own web. Her mind sent out feelers in all directions, searching. Then she smiled "An old friend. Drew. Yes, I'm in love with Drew."

"Oh!"

Corliss got to her feet. "You must rest now, Jennie. Have I told you everything you want to know?"

Jennie clenched Corliss's hand tightly, squeezing it feverishly. "You've no idea what you've just given me, Corliss. Oh, thank you, thank you!"

"Stop doubting Reese. He's a good man. An honest man."

"Yes," Jennie said, smiling happily. "He is. And he loves me! He really loves me."

Corliss couldn't bear it another moment. She said goodbye and left quickly. Now, riding back to the lab in the taxi, she wondered how she had been able to lie so convincingly. But she had. This time, surely, a lie was justified. Jennie had needed to hear it so badly. How could I have done anything else? Corliss asked herself. How could I?

XXV

Corliss found it difficult to concentrate the rest of the day. When five o'clock came, she decided to stay and complete her reports.

"You needn't do that," Paul told her.

"I'd rather. Please. I – want to stay."

"Burr's upset you."

"Not Burr so much. He always upsets me. But it was Jennie. Paul, the chances are she's not going to get well. All the tests indicate that."

"I know."

"She's so young. It's not fair!"

"Strange talk for a girl who lost her man to her," Paul said.

"I know," Corliss said with a smile. "I suppose it is. But I felt so sorry for her – please, let's not talk about her anymore."

"If you want to stay, do so. I'm going home for a little while, but I'll be back.

Okay?"

Corliss was glad when Paul had gone. She phoned home to tell Martha that she would be staying, and for the next hour she worked in the quiet lab, trying hard to concentrate on what she was doing. But it was difficult. At last, she decided to take a break and come back a little later. She met Paul just returning as she left. She took half an hour for a sandwich which she couldn't eat, but drank two cups of coffee. Returning to the lab, she saw a light burning in Paul's office and went there. She stepped inside.

"Paul—"

She froze in her tracks.

"Come in, Miss Mitchell!"

Paul was in his chair behind the desk, holding tightly to the arms of it, looking white and angry. Beside him was a tall, thin man. A man with a moustache. The man she had seen at the mill, and once on the road! Again at Sadie's Place. The man she had suspected was the prowler of Willow Woods. Cassiday!

"What is this? What's going on?"

she asked.

Cassiday raised an old-fashioned pistol. She recognized it immediately. It was the same one Mrs. Petrie had been slipping into her basket that day in Drew's kitchen!

"Don't be fooled by this. It shoots very straight and very deadly. It's unfortunate that you came back when you did. You leave me no alternative. You'll come with us now."

Cassiday motioned to Paul to stand up. Paul had a long cardboard tube in his hands.

"Paul, your drawings!"

"It seems we're being escorted somewhere by this young man. It has to do with Unit One."

"Move," Cassiday said. "There's a car out in back. Get in it. Act natural. Don't try anything."

There was nothing to do but go. The car was waiting. Cassiday ordered them into the back seat, then he took the wheel, and they sped through town and out to the open highway. Soon, Corliss saw that

335

they were going in the general direction of Willow Woods.

"You've been living in Willow Woods, haven't you?" she asked. "First at the mill, then at Millard's place."

"Yeah, something like that," Cassiday said.

"You're the prowler people have been seeing, you're the man who's been stealing things!"

"Petty thefts," he laughed crudely. "Until I won enough at a poker game at Sadie's Place to set me up in fine style. Until I got a certain engineer under my thumb."

Corliss closed her eyes. Tom Whittier! Was that why Tom had been so slow in developing Unit Two? Because he was a part of the plot?

"You'll never get away with it," Corliss said. "Never in a million years. Paul's already gone to the patent office."

Cassiday laughed. "But there's been delays. The big man pulled a few strings, just to hold things up."

"So you think you can steal my plans

and claim the design for yourselves!" Paul said dismally.

"Only you played it cute, mister. You left something out. Kept it in your head. Now the blasted thing won't work."

"Naturally." Paul nodded. "I'm no fool."

Soon, Cassiday was twisting the wheel, and they bounced off the road. They were in the north end of the woods. It had been some time since Corliss had been in this general area. The lane was nearly impassable and very narrow. Then they stopped, and Cassiday moved some brush that hid a gate. They drove through, and Cassiday put the brush back in place.

"Camouflage," Paul said. "They seem to have thought of everything."

Cassiday was back. The car lurched forward again. In a few minutes, they had reached a small cottage. Corliss remembered it. It had once been a summer home. For years now it had been empty. Corliss remembered the people who had once spent their summers here.

At the door, Cassiday gave three

knocks. The door opened, and Cassiday pushed them inside. Tom Whittier was there, a stricken look on his face. In a large room, two pieces of equipment were in evidence, partially torn down, wires and small parts strewn everywhere.

"You've got both units!" Paul said with surprise. "How—"

Cassiday rubbed his fingers together. "We lifted Unit Two out of Mitchell Enterprises tonight. Tom's been working on Unit One. Now get busy. Put it together. Quick."

"How could you, Tom?" Corliss asked. "How could you?"

"Cut the gab," Cassiday said angrily. "Where's Ma? I'm starving."

Tom handed Paul a few tools. "Better do what he says, Paul. Show me what's wrong. What have you left out?"

Corliss couldn't believe this was happening. It was a nightmare. She kept watching Tom. Her father had believed in him! He was the best engineer at Mitchell Electronics! How could he have betrayed them like this?

Paul tossed off his jacket and bent to the task. Perspiration made a dark stain on his shirt between his shoulders.

The nightmare wore on and on like a movie in slow motion. The cottage was airless. Cassiday went several times to peer out the window. "I'm starving," he complained.

"Maybe something's gone wrong," Tom said.

"Shut up!" Cassiday said nervously. "Nothing's going to go wrong!"

"I heard something," Corliss said.

"Yeah. It's okay. There's the signal."

Paul glanced at Corliss. Her nerves jumped. She knew what he was trying to say with his eyes. Cassiday went to open the door. Paul leaped with a football tackle, and the two men rolled on the floor. Corliss sprang for the light switch, and everything went dark. The old pistol exploded with a flash of light. Corliss screamed. Then two strong arms were around her. It was Tom.

"Fool! Fool! Don't try anything!" he said in a harsh whisper.

The lights came on. Paul was on the floor, shaking his head groggily. Cassiday snatched up the pistol where it had fallen. The bullet had gone wild, plowing into the facing around the door.

"What's going on?"

Corliss stared with disbelief. She knew that voice. "Alex! Alex Ward."

He stepped inside. When he saw her, he was angry. "What's she doing here?"

"Had to bring her," Cassiday shrugged. "She came barging into the lab when I was picking up Gilman."

"Of all the idiot things—"

"Too late now," Cassiday drawled. "What's it matter? In a few hours, we'll all be out here. Have you got the payoff?"

Alex shook his head. "No payoff until we deliver the goods in working order. You know that as well as I do!"

"It's all adding up now," Corliss said wearily. "This is why you kept taking Elizabeth out. She must have given you some information you needed."

"Sure," Alex said. "All about Paul's Unit One. Where he kept the plans—and

340

about Unit Two as well. I got an idea. A big idea. It smelled like money and I like money."

Corliss held her head. What was going to happen once Paul got the units working? She didn't want to think about it. These men were playing for high stakes. There was still one more man. The boss. The man who would pay them for stealing the plans. She could guess who it was.

There were three short knocks at the door. "Son? You in there?"

Cassiday laughed. "It's only Ma. At last! I'm darned near starved."

Cassiday opened the door. Mrs. Petrie walked in, a basket over her arm.

Cassiday put his arm around Mrs. Petrie. "This is my ma," he said, nodding to Corliss. "I'm Ben. Ben Petrie. . . . Now, what you got in there, Ma?"

Just as Mrs. Petrie was about to leave, the door burst open. Cassiday and Alex reached for their guns, but they were too late. The sheriff was there with Drew right behind him.

"Easy now, boys," the sheriff said.

"I've got men all around the place. I'd suggest all of you come peacefully."

"Thank God!" Tom said. "I didn't think you'd ever get here, Drew."

"We made it, Tom," Drew said. "And you deserve a lot of the credit."

Alex lunged for Tom, but Drew intervened. He held Alex back. "It's all over, Alex," Drew said. "Tom played it close, but he played it right for a change. For what he did to help us, all is forgiven."

"You mean that, Drew?" Tom asked. "How can you ever trust me again?"

"I think you've learned your lesson," Drew smiled.

Corliss watched the sheriff take Alex Ward and Ben Petrie alias Cassiday into custody. Mrs. Petrie was taken, too.

"But how did you know where to come, Drew?" Corliss asked.

"Tom told us to follow Mrs. Petrie tonight when she brought the food basket. So we did. Are you all right, Corliss? When your father told me you were staying late at the lab, I tried to reach you there to warn you, but I was too late."

"I'm fine," Corliss said. "But it's been a very, very long day. Take me home, Drew."

"Sure, brat. Sure."

He came to put his arm around her, and together they walked away from the summer cottage and out into the night.

XXVI

The story made the front page of the Sea-bourne paper the next morning. Burr Kaldner's name did not appear. The sheriff had no proof that Burr was to have been the recipient of the stolen equipment. He'd been clever, as usual. It was Ben Petrie and Alex Ward's word against Burr's, and Burr had too much influence. But the whispers were everywhere. Everyone knew.

It was that same day that Corliss had a phone call at the lab.

"Corliss, this is Reese."

Before he told her, she guessed what had happened.

"It's Jennie. We've lost her," he said. "About an hour ago."

When the line went dead, she remembered the stark echo of his voice ringing in her ears. So, it was over now. Poor Jennie didn't have to suffer anymore. Corliss turned away from the phone, tears in her eyes. Elizabeth saw them and knew.

The funeral was a large one. To Corliss's surprise, her father insisted upon going.

"Burr's my enemy. But he loved Jennie. Everyone knew that. I pity him."

Jennie was laid to rest in a cemetery in the country within sight of green fields and white fences, where horses grazed and romped with colts. It was a fitting place for Jennie. As Corliss listened to the last words being said at the service, she was aware of the tall pine trees, the wind stirring the upper branches. It was unseasonably warm, and the wind seemed almost hot. She remembered thinking, Why does the wind always have to blow at times like this?

After the service, they saw Burr briefly. Corliss shook his big hand and saw that something had died inside him. It was in his eyes, his face, the tone of his voice. Reese hid behind dark glasses, a tall, quiet man with an unreadable face. He barely acknowledged her words of sympathy.

Returning to Seabourne, Corliss went to the lab. Father decided to go to the plant, his first real visit there since his illness.

Corliss found the lab very quiet. Empty. "Elizabeth –" She heard voices down the hall and going to Paul's office, she glanced in. "Oh!"

Elizabeth was in Paul's arms. With a laugh, Elizabeth sprang away. Paul blushed. "Sorry. We didn't hear you," Paul said.

"Don't apologize. I hope this means what I think it means."

"It does," Paul nodded. "I've asked her to marry me. She's accepted."

"I never knew I could be so happy, Corliss," Elizabeth said.

"I think it's wonderful! I can't think of two nicer people for this to happen to," Corliss said.

"I'm going back to Washington in a few days," Paul said. "It might make a nice honeymoon trip. Could you manage things here?''

"Of course!''

Later, working beside Elizabeth in the lab, Corliss asked about Alex.

"It was over with him. That last date proved it. It's a good thing considering how everything turned out. I never dreamed Alex would stoop so low—''

"That's past history,'' Corliss pointed out.

"I knew he was asking a lot of questions about the lab and Paul. But I was just foolish enough to think he was interested because of me. Oh, Corliss, I've been such a fool—''

"But it's over. And there's Paul.''

"Paul,'' Elizabeth smiled. "Sweet, dear, Paul! Sometimes, I think I've loved him for a long time and didn't realize it. Could that be?''

"Yes,'' she said. And for some reason she couldn't pin-point, Drew Fielding crossed her mind.

A week later, Paul and Elizabeth were married in a quiet ceremony. Corliss kissed them both and sent them on their way. She was glad for the work at the lab. There was plenty of it. Working alone called for long, long hours. She welcomed them. She thought often of Reese. Occasionally, she heard something about him. He did not phone or come by. But he would. She was certain of it. In time. He was free again. She knew she must not think about such things, but she couldn't help it. She knew the moment would come, eventually, when she must meet his green eyes and hear what he would say.

It was late one evening when she heard a knock at the laboratory door and went to answer it. "Who is it?"

"Burr Kaldner. I would like to speak with you, Corliss."

She was so stunned that for a moment she couldn't believe her ears. Then, fumbling with the lock, she opened the door. Burr stepped into the lab. He looked out of place here, a big bearish man with the inevitable cigar in his hand.

"How are you, Burr?"

His face was haggard. He looked as if he had not slept in days. "I miss Jennie."

"Of course you do. She was a sweet girl."

"A fine girl. She thought her father was the world itself, did you know that?" He raised tear-filld eyes. "Corliss, did she know about me? Do you think she could have known about – about Paul's equipment – about – you know –"

"I don't know, Burr."

"I wish I knew! She said something funny that last day. Something the very morning the story was in the paper. She said –" he paused for a moment, voice breaking. "She said, 'Daddy, how could you? How could you?' Do you think she meant that, do you think –"

"She was very ill. How could she have heard?"

"The nurses were probably talking about it. They were all gossips. Maybe she heard something on the radio. She had one beside her bed."

"She loved you, Burr. Just remember that."

"But I disappointed her! I let her see what kind of man I really was! I never let her know that before until it was too late to change it for her. Until it was too late –'' Burr got control of himself at last. "I'm sorry I bothered you, Corliss. I guess I really came to thank you for what you did for Jennie that day. You lied to her, didn't you? About Reese loving her when he married her."

"Yes, I lied. I only pray she believed me."

"For Jennie, I thank you," Burr said. "She believed you. I know she did."

Then he was gone, and the lab seemed very quiet. Corliss moved to the window and watched Burr's big car drive away.

It was a few days later when Corliss managed to leave the lab early for a change and drive home at twilight. She found Drew's car in front of the house. He was on the terrace with her father, deep in conversation.

"Hi," she called. "What's up?"

Drew got to his feet. He was smiling. "The most unbelievable thing has happened!"

Father was beaming. "It's Burr. He's

offered to sell out his company to us."

"Burr!" she said, startled.

"He wants out. He's going away. Taking a long trip somewhere. He has enough money, so he doesn't need to work. The fight's gone out of him."

"Are we buying?"

"We're buying," Drew nodded.

"What about Reese?"

Drew gave her a long look. "He can stay if he wants. Not as a vice-president, but in a good, reliable position."

"What has he decided?"

"I don't know," Drew said.

Drew stayed for dinner. Then, with a bulging briefcase under his arm, he said goodnight and drove away.

Father was in a splendid mood. He was elated as Corliss hadn't seen him in a long time. "Oh, by the way, Corliss, Madeline Huffman called. They're going to open the mill to the public next month. She wanted you to know. Have you seen it lately?"

"No, I haven't."

"I walked down the other day. It's

quite impressive. You should go and take a look."

"Yes. Perhaps I will."

Why not now? It was just dusk. But she knew the way, and there were no longer prowlers to worry about. The evenings were growing cooler. There was autumn color in the trees, and leaves were falling. The skies were deeper, and the sunsets redder. It was her favorite time of the year. And Christmas. She loved Christmas in the woods! With Drew to help, she always searched for a tree that was just right. Then Drew would cut it for her, and together, laughing and clowning, they would drag it through the snow to the house. They would decorate it, using all the old familiar ornaments, and later, before a roaring fire, they would drink hot chocolate and munch Christmas cookies. It was so much fun. A tradition really. A part of her.

The mill stood in the golden glow of sunset, a magnificent memento of yesterday. The restoration had erased the rotted wood and braced the sagging roof. But it hadn't spoiled it. It was just as lovely as it had always been.

"Corliss—"

She started. He stood in the shadows, but she saw him, and she knew every familiar line of him. "Reese!"

He came toward her. A tall man. With thick black hair and green eyes and very white teeth. He looked tired, and for the first time, she saw a touch of gray at his temples.

"How are you, Corliss?"

"I'm all right. And you?"

"It's been hell. In many ways."

"I know. Poor Jennie."

"Poor Jennie," he murmured.

"You made her happy."

"I tried. I truly tried."

"There will be a star in your crown for that."

"No," he shook his head. "I deserve nothing. I married Jennie in return for the vice-presidency. It was a cut-and-dried business deal with Burr."

Corliss shrank back.

"You knew. Deep down you always

knew," Reese said.

She couldn't find her voice.

"When we were kids, I told you I'd be somebody someday," Reese said. "One way or another. But what do I have now? Jennie's gone. Burr's gone. I'm nobody again."

"Oh, Reese, that's ridiculous! How can you say that?"

"Because it's true. Oh, I know. Drew offered me a job. A good job. It was decent of him. He owed me nothing. If the positions had been reversed, I wouldn't have done as much for him."

"You're being too hard on yourself."

"Someone has to be," he said with a wry smile. "I'm going away, Corliss. I've got a job on the West Coast. A good job. It has a future. I'll come back someday soon. Will you be waiting?"

She lifted her head. She took a good, long, hard look at this man she had always loved. He reached out to touch her. He touched her. And nothing happened. She took his hand and held it for a moment. "No, Reese, I won't be waiting."

They stared at each other. He opened his lips as if to protest. Then he nodded slowly. "It died the night I told you I was going to marry Jennie, didn't it?"

"I think it would have died anyway, Reese. With or without Jennie."

"Can't you forgive me?"

"I already have."

"Corliss—"

He put his arms around her, and for the last time, he held her, and she put her cheek against his shoulder. He brushed her hair with his lips.

"I've been such a fool. But I was always stubborn. I always had to learn the hard way. Can't we try again?"

She shook her head. "No."

"You represent a big chunk of my life."

"And you a big part of mine," she answered.

"What went wrong?" he asked with despair. "What?"

"Too much."

"Yes," he sighed. "Too much."

"I hope you'll find what you want,

Reese, somewhere, someday.''

She kissed him, lightly, sweetly, on the lips. He let her go then. He knew it was over. Just as she knew.

Reese moved away. At the edge of the woods, he paused and stood there for a moment looking back at her, at the old mill, the reflection in the green pool. He lifted his head and looked at the trees and the sky. When he turned back, he gave her a pensive, wistful smile. "I never did belong here."

Then he was gone. She heard his footsteps crushing the fallen leaves, the sound of his car starting and driving away.

She wept. For all the golden, beautiful memories that were here. For all that had happened to them both. For a long time, she sat on an old log where she and Reese had sat so often in the past, and stared at the mill as the moon came out and put silver edges around the wheel and kissed the weathered roof.

At last she bent down and, with cupped hands, scooped up the cool water from the

pool. She bathed her face. She began to feel better. She began to think of other things.

XXVII

Corliss kept her days filled. Paul and Elizabeth returned from their Washington honeymoon with good news concerning Paul's patent. Production could begin on his equipment, and Drew was rushing it along.

At times, Corliss would pause in the middle of an experiment or between bites of a sandwich or awaken from a dream at night and wonder why she had said no to Reese. When had she known she no longer loved him? She could not exactly pinpoint it. Reese had been a part of her life so long. Had loving him simply become a habit? She didn't know.

There were no more tears. She was not sad nor was she happy. She walked through the days, somewhere in between, wondering at herself and asking herself why a dozen times a day.

Roberts Mill was opened to the public, but without the good graces of Madeline Huffman. As quickly as she had appeared in Willow Woods, she had gone. Corliss asked Drew about it, when they attended the dedication services. "Why did she leave? Who was she?"

"She was someone I knew. Someone I once loved. She thought now that her husband was dead, it might work for us."

"But it didn't?"

"No, brat, it didn't," Drew said with a slow smile. "No more than it worked for you and Reese. It is over with Reese, isn't it?"

"Yes."

He lifted her chin and looked deep into her eyes. "How do you feel about that, Corliss?"

"I don't know when I stopped loving Reese. Perhaps a long time ago. Perhaps only yesterday. I only know I no longer love him. So much happened to us. Always it was something that drove a wedge between us. From the beginning, it was that way. It was never meant to be, Drew."

359

"I tried to tell you that once."

She smiled and nodded. "I know. I should have listened." She was aware of the sun on his big face, the rumpled way the wind had left his hair. "Is it really over with Madeline, Drew?"

"It never began," he said. "Aren't you going to ask me why?"

She gave him a quick, teasing smile. "All right, why?"

He took her face in his big hands. He smoothed back her hair and traced the outline of her jaw, the shape of her lips. Her pulse gave a queer, excited leap. He had never touched her like this before. He had never looked at her with such a warm light in his eyes. "It's because I love someone else."

A wave of shock swept over her. "Oh!"

"Aren't you going to ask who?" His gray eyes were so tender. His lips lifted into a smile. "You, Corliss. It's always been you!"

She stared at him. He laughed softly and put his arm around her shoulders. "Come along now, let's join the others.

The program is about to begin.''

Somehow, she got through the dedication. She applauded the speakers. She smiled at her neighbors and spoke with friends, but did it all automatically. For her heart was consumed with the look she had seen in Drew's eyes. She shivered as she remembered his touch. His words echoed through her heart, consumed her mind, rippled along her nerves. Drew loved her!

In the crowd, they became separated. He seemed to be avoiding her. It was just as well. He knew it would take time for her to get used to the idea. Drew – in love with her!

The autumn days slipped along. Corliss worked hard at the lab and helped Paul with his research. She knew Drew was very busy at the plant, consolidating all of Burr Kaldner's properties into Mitchell Electronics.

Mrs. Petrie, of course, was gone, and Drew didn't replace her. He came often to dinner and lingered long after her father

361

had retired. On a frosty night in the middle of October, when he whistled for Fuzz and prepared to leave, he pulled her close. He kissed her for the first time, warmly, tenderly, and with an ardor that surprised her.

"Not yet, Drew. Please, not yet—"

"All right."

But the kiss had been the first of the fires he set off in her heart. It burned there, growing steadily. She found herself planning her days around Drew. She thought up excuses to see and be near him. Then one day, she realized that it had always been this way. She had always flown to Drew when she needed something, when anything went wrong. Why else had she gone to him when she needed sustaining? Why else had his home been like her own? Why else had she been so comfortable there, so at peace. Why else?

It had been nearly three months since Reese had gone. She no longer missed him. When she thought of him at all, it was with no real regret or sorrow. Only in a nostalgic misty way.

Christmas was just around the corner, and she was in a festive mood. The day came that traditionally Drew helped her fetch a tree from the woods.

She pulled on snow boots, wrapped a scarf around her hair, tugged on a warm coat, and struck out along the path. The woods, bare now of leaves, were still beautiful. She saw rabbit tracks in the snow and caught sight of a deer near Drew's house. She hurried toward the gate. Fuzz saw her. He came barking to greet her. Drew appeared, stepping out in his shirt sleeves. "Hi!" he called.

With a laugh, she reached down for a fistful of snow, fashioned a large snowball, and hurled it at him. He ducked. Then he came charging after her. Fuzz got into the game, circling them and barking. Drew shouted at her, and she laughed as she ran. At last, Drew caught her and picked her up in his big arms and held her fast. "There's a snowbank over there. Which will it be? That or a kiss?"

She stopped laughing. His gray eyes held hers. She reached up to brush the snow out of his brown hair. "Oh, Drew—"

The light deepened in his eyes. He carried her inside the house and to the den where a fire blazed on the hearth. She loved the warm flames, the cozy room, the snowy, beautiful day outside. And she loved this man.

"Don't put me down, Drew. Hold me. Don't ever put me down!"

"Not a chance! I've waited too long."

A log dropped on the fire, throwing sparks. She saw a few flakes of snow beginning to fall beyond the window. She thought of the Christmas tree—fleetingly. But it could wait. There were more important things to do right now.

She kissed him then. Not as a sister, not as an old friend, or even a new friend. But as a woman in love.